UNFRIENDLY
COMPETITION

Other books in the
CANTERWOOD CREST SERIES:

CANTERWOOD
CREST

UNFRIENDLY
COMPETITION

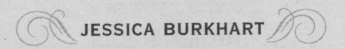

JESSICA BURKHART

ALADDIN M!X
New York London Toronto Sydney

J
FIC
BURKHAR
2011

This book is a work of fiction. Any references to historical events, real people, or real locales are used fictitiously. Other names, characters, places, and incidents are the product of the author's imagination, and any resemblance to actual events or locales or persons, living or dead, is entirely coincidental.

ALADDIN M!X

Simon & Schuster Children's Publishing Division

1230 Avenue of the Americas, New York, NY 10020

First Aladdin M!X edition January 2011

Copyright © 2011 by Jessica Burkhart

All rights reserved, including the right of reproduction
in whole or in part in any form.

ALADDIN is a trademark of Simon & Schuster, Inc., and related logo
is a registered trademark of Simon & Schuster, Inc.

ALADDIN M!X and related logo are registered trademarks
of Simon & Schuster, Inc

For information about special discounts for bulk purchases, please
contact Simon & Schuster Special Sales at 1-866-506-1949
or business@simonandschuster.com.

The Simon & Schuster Speakers Bureau can bring authors to your live event.
For more information or to book an event contact the Simon & Schuster Speakers
Bureau at 1-866-248-3049 or visit our website at www.simonspeakers.com.

Designed by Jessica Handelman

The text of this book was set in Venetian 301 BT.

Manufactured in the United States of America 1210 OFF

2 4 6 8 10 9 7 5 3 1

Library of Congress Control Number 2010940034

ISBN 978-1-4424-0386-4

ISBN 978-1-4424-0387-1 (eBook)

To everyone who helped Sasha make the journey
from the first book to now. I can't express how grateful I am.

ACKNOWLEDGMENTS

A huge thanks to the Simon & Schuster team including Fiona Simpson, Bethany Buck, Mara Anastas, Liesa Abrams, Jessica Handelman, Venessa Williams, and Bess Braswell (miss you both!), Lucille Rettino, Katherine Devendorf, Alyson Heller, Ellen Chan, Karin Paprocki, Russell Gordon, Dayna Evans, and supereditor Kate Angelella.

Kate, your wonderful ideas and thoughtful edits made Sasha's end-of-reign at Canterwood an amazing one. Canterwood would not have made it to this book without you—no doubt. You're the dream editor that authors wish they had. (But I'm totally territorial, fellow authors, ahem . . .) I can't even begin to thank you enough for being there for Sasha's final moments as narrator.

Ross Angelella, thank you for being a source of support though writing this book and much more.

Bonne Belle, it wasn't hard to mention lip gloss, oh, at least a zillion times throughout the book.

Team Canterwood, you are the heart of these books. I can't begin to thank you enough for all you do! xo

While writing this book, I learned a lot about what priorities really are and what is important. My perspectives on a lot of things have changed.

Kate, by the time you're reading this in book format, a new year will have just begun. We'll be signing a new pop song that will annoy everyone around us, have enough Silly Bandz to fill a small closet, and will have outfitted ourselves with everything possible from Hello Kitty. ^_^ LYSSM. <33

UNFRIENDLY COMPETITION

I

TWO WEEKS
NOTICE

"WILL THE FOLLOWING STUDENTS PLEASE report to the headmistress' office: Heather Fox, Alison Robb, Julia Myer, and Sasha Silver."

The loudspeaker silenced and I jerked up my head. Why was *I* being called to the office? My palms instantly started to sweat and my pink, sparkly Bic pen became slick in my fingers as I kept scribbling in my math notebook, hoping I'd imagined the announcement.

"Sasha, go ahead," Ms. Utz said. "I'll be sure one of your classmates fills you in about the weekend's homework."

Um, guess not.

"I'll get your homework," Brit whispered, leaning toward me. Her almond-shaped eyes were framed by nervous, pushed-together eyebrows, but I could tell she was trying to hide her worry. Probably to help me from getting more scared than I already was. "Text me when you're out of Drake's office—I know you'll be fine."

I nodded, gathering my notebook, pen, textbook, and butter-soft brown messenger bag that I'd borrowed from Brit. As my BFF and roomie, she had calmed me a little.

But note: only a *little*.

I slung my bag over my shoulder, stepping around desks, and walked out of the math classroom, closing the door behind me. The second I got outside, my phone buzzed.

It was a BlackBerry Messenger conversation. And Alison, Julia, and Heather were already talking. The Trio wasn't wasting a second dissecting the sitch before we got to Headmistress Drake's. I opened the talk.

Alison Robb:

Why r we being called?☹

Julia Myer:

Who knows. We didn't do ANYTHING. Don't worry.

Heather Fox:

'Course we didn't. Silver? Where r u? Were u wearing earplugs when the impossibly-loud announcement was made?

Geez! I started typing.

Sasha Silver:

I heard it, H. I'm in math and on the way 2 the admin bldg. Where r u guys? Wanna meet up and go 2gether?

Heather Fox:

We def should. Let's all meet at the courtyard ASAP.

Alison Robb:

K. Glad 2 go w u guys. Nervous.

Julia Myer:

BRT.

I closed the conversation and shoved my cotton-candy-pink BlackBerry into my bag. I pushed open the glass door of the math building and hurried out into the early November air. It was already cold outside, but anxiety made me even chillier. I tugged down my scarlet-colored cable-knit sweater and buttoned my black wool coat, shoving my hands in the pockets.

I made my way across the empty campus and hurried to the courtyard. The cobblestone circle with its fountain and stone benches was only a couple of minutes from the admin building.

Boots clicked on the cobblestones, arms looped together, Heather and Alison walked up to me.

"Any idea what this is about?" I asked, assuming that if anyone knew anything it would be Heather Fox.

She shook her soft blond hair. "Nope. But I'm not worried. At least, not for myself." She shifted her blue eyes to me, then to Alison. "*I* didn't do anything."

"Me either!" Alison's normally soft voice was loud. She ran her fingers through her sandy brown hair like she always did when she was worried. "I just want to go and get it over with. Where's Julia?"

Alison started to pull her phone out of her camel-colored Burberry coat. But just as she did, Julia came around the corner a few yards away and walked up to us.

Her angled blond bob had two pieces twisted back with tiny purple flower clips with rhinestones (actually, probably diamonds) in the centers.

"We've been waiting for, like, five minutes," Heather snapped.

"Sorry." Julia shrank for a second, then recovered. "I was in the middle of a history pop quiz. I had to finish before I left."

Heather waved off the excuse with her butter yellow leather-gloved hand. "Whatever. Let's go."

The four of us left the courtyard and our boots crunched on the grass, dried by the weeks of cold air. The administration building loomed in front of us, looking imposing like the rest of campus. Even though

I'd been at Canterwood Crest Academy over a year, there hadn't been a time when I didn't notice the prestigious, gorgeous campus.

Until now. My nerves wouldn't allow me to do anything but look straight ahead.

We reached the administration building waaay too soon. Even Heather, the fearless Canterwood Queen Bee, paused for a second before stepping up the stairs flanked by spiky black iron railings.

Alison, Julia, and I followed her inside, and I sighed to myself, glad for the heat that blasted us when we walked inside. We followed the gold plaques pointing to the headmistress's office and stopped in front of her secretary's desk.

Mrs. Kratz, who might have been here when Canterwood was started in the eighteen hundreds, looked up at us through horn-rimmed glasses.

"I'm Heather Fox, and we're here to see Headmistress Drake."

There wasn't a waver in Heather's voice. She sounded as if she was ordering movie tickets.

"Ah, yes. Ms. Drake is expecting all of you now. Go right in."

Julia turned first, and Heather, Alison, and I followed

her across the room to the headmistress's glossy wooden door. Without pause, Julia knocked on the door. The sound seemed to echo in the tiny hallway.

"Come in."

The headmistress's voice came from behind the closed door. My mouth was so dry, I couldn't even swallow. The headmistress was *scary*.

Julia turned the brass knob and we filed inside behind her. Headmistress Drake, seated in a large, leather office chair behind her desk finished writing on her notepad before glancing up at us. With minimal makeup, a buttoned black blouse and half-carat diamond studs, she looked every bit the headmistress of an elite East Coast boarding school.

Her black hair was pulled into a tight bun, and she was sleek, but looked like she could take somebody down. Ms. Drake's pale skin looked even more delicate against her red lipstick.

She didn't offer any of us a chair and none of us moved to sit. We stood in front of her—waiting.

Headmistress Drake looked at us for what felt like hours. "I know one of you created the gossip blog."

I tried not to let my knees shake.

"The school's technology department did some research and narrowed it down to a certain building—Orchard

Hall. With even further investigation, we were able to find Internet protocol addresses that matched two rooms."

Headmistress Drake looked at the Trio. "Your suite." Then she looked at me. "And your room with Brit Chan."

"None of us—" Alison started, stopping when Headmistress Drake cut her off with a shake of her head.

"I have proof, Miss Robb. The only reason I did not call Miss Chan here is because she is a new student and does not have the insight on campus that the blogger does. So, there are two options for the four of you."

I felt as if I'd been punched in the stomach. There was no way one of us had created that dumb gossip blog. The blog that ridiculed the school and made up awful rumors. I hadn't and the Trio was too smart for that.

I glanced at Heather, noticing her eyes were focused to the side for a brief second before she shifted her gaze back to the headmistress.

"You have the choice to step forward and tell me who created the blog," Headmistress Drake said.

Not one of us moved.

"Or, you will *all* be expelled from Canterwood Crest Academy unless I learn the truth. I'm giving you one week, then I'm telling your parents."

2
EMERGENCY MEETING

"TEXT BRIT AND TELL HER TO MEET US AT our suite" were the only words Heather spoke as we walked back to Orchard. Since we'd all been in our final class of the day, Headmistress Drake had told us to go back to our rooms. Meaning: no afternoon riding lesson for us. We'd been sent back to Orchard and the head-mistress said she'd notify Mr. Conner of our absence.

"This is *ridiculous!*" Julia yelled, slamming the Trio's door behind us when we got inside.

Brit, glancing at all of us, had no clue what had happened.

"First, the random accusation and now we can't even go to our lesson today?" Julia continued. "What is she thinking?"

"You can't ride?" Brit asked, still standing near the door. "Why?" Unlike the rest of us, Brit was dressed in breeches, glossy Ariat boots, and a button-down riding shirt.

"Apparently, one of us created the gossip blog," I told her. "Headmistress Drake said one of us has two weeks to confess or we're *all* going to be expelled."

Brit couldn't mask the shock on her face. Her dark brown eyes opened wide, and she flipped her long black French braid over her shoulder. "*What?*"

"The tech department traced the blog's IP to our rooms," I said, flopping on the Trio's couch. "But that's impossible. How could they get that so wrong?"

"If they tracked it to our rooms, why didn't I get called into the office?" Brit asked.

"Newbie card," Alison said, her cheeks still pink from the cold or embarrassment—I wasn't sure. "The headmistress thought the blog was too rooted in Canterwood history for someone so new to write it."

Heather couldn't sit. She paced around the Trio's living room before planting her hands on one of the recliners.

"No one's confessing anything." She looked at Brit. "And you need to get to the stable. Unlike the rest of us, *you're* still riding today."

Brit glanced at me. "I don't want to leave when you've got this going on."

"You have to," I said. "You don't have an excuse. Go or you'll get in trouble. I'll fill you in when you get back."

"Okay," Brit said, finally. She stepped backward toward the door. "I'm so sorry, guys. But we'll figure it out and prove that none of you did it."

Alison, chewing her cheek, nodded. "I hope so."

Brit left and it hit me that I wasn't going to see Charm, my Thoroughbred-Belgian gelding, tonight. Sadness turned to anger. I hadn't done anything. Neither had the Trio.

"What are we going to do?" I asked.

Heather, who had finally sat down, looked up at me from her cross-legged position on the carpet. Julia kept playing with her phone, and Alison wrapped herself tighter in her pool blue throw blanket.

"I'm *definitely* not going to sit around and hope who-ever did it goes to the headmistress," Heather said. "I've worked *way* too hard to get here. There's not a chance that I'm going to let someone mess with my future, especially when it comes to riding. I'm *not* missing Huntington because some bored, pathetic person decided to spill their guts on the Internet."

Huntington Stables. *The* Huntington Classic. I'd been so focused on the e-word—expulsion—that I'd forgotten about the biggest, most important event in my career as a rider. My first major horse show as a rider on the Youth Equestrian National Team—the most difficult riding program in the country. If anyone could figure this out, it would be Heather. But that didn't mean I wasn't nervous. If we were expelled, we wouldn't be going to the classic.

And we'd never see Canterwood again.

3
PARTY PLANNERS, INC.

LAZY SATURDAY MORNINGS WERE MY favorite. Brit was cross-legged on the floor, going through her crazy sock collection.

I peered over my bed, staring at her. "What *are* you looking for?"

Brit shrugged, her attention still on her socks. "Something fun to wear under my black boots."

She had way more than a dozen pairs of socks—rainbows, hearts, all colors of stripes and polka dots. I loved this about Brit: She dressed like a catalog model, but wore something fun under her jeans or shoes that no one saw. It was an unexpected and cool departure from her überchic outfits.

"I love the red and black striped ones," I said. "They're so pretty and very fall-like."

We were both getting ready, slowly, to go to the Trio's suite. Our phones had buzzed at the same minute. It had been a text from Heather. She'd invited Brit and me over to her suite to chill—or, and, as she'd put it in the text, "Get over here 2 plan my epic bday party. Ur already late."

Brit and I had just shaken our heads then started to get ready. Heather's thirteenth birthday was nothing to mess with. Thirteen was a big deal. And I was sure until *the* date—November tenth—Heather would be making sure she got the blowout she wanted.

Brit pulled on her pair of socks—the red and black ones I'd suggested—and my phone buzzed. BBM.

Jacob Schwartz:

How's ur morning?

I hurried to type back. Just seeing his name pop up on my BBM made me feel all fluttery.

Sasha Silver:

Good! Brit and I r abt 2 go 2 Trio's suite.

Jacob Schwartz:

Why?

Sasha Silver:

Heather invited us over to plan her 13th bday. It's on Weds.

Jacob Schwartz:

Ohhh. Man. Did u ever think *U'd* be planning her bday?

Sasha Silver:

LOL. Um, not rlly. But you know how our friendship has changed, so I'm actually excited. Got to run, but talk later?

Jacob Schwartz:

Def. ☺ Maybe over hot chocolate @ SS?

Sasha Silver:

<3 to. TTYL.

I stopped typing and glanced up. Brit, still on the floor, was grinning up at me.

"That wasn't, oh, I don't know . . . Jacob," she taunted. "Was it?"

I put my phone in my purse, unable to stop my smile.

"He wanted to know what we were doing," I said. "I told him about Heather's party. And he wants to meet up tonight."

Brit stood, pulling on knee-high boots. "Yay! And it's going to be the party of the year. Maybe of the decade. I know I haven't been here long, but I can't imagine there's going to be a party even close to the one that's about to happen this week."

I smoothed my comfy purple VS Pink yoga pants and put a hoodie over my black shirt that looked as if it had been dusted with fine glitter.

Brit and I left our room and walked to the Trio's

suite. Someone, probably artsy Alison, had decorated the door with fall decorations. A beautiful wreath of bright-colored fall leaves hung above their white board. Above and around the doorway, a string of soft white lights made their suite look fall-ready.

Brit knocked and, seconds later, Julia pulled open the door. She was dressed in riding clothes and there was a look of annoyance—something that had seemed perma-nent since YENT tryouts—on her face.

"Hey," Brit and I said, stepping inside. We went for the small couch in their living room and sat down. I loved the Trio's cozy suite. A liquid potpourri holder gave off wafts of pumpkin spice in the air. Like always, the place was spotless and the flat-screen TV was muted on an entertainment channel.

"Hi." Julia's response was short. She picked up her MacBook Air off the couch, slamming the lid shut. She looked comfy in cropped leggings and an oversize red sweater. "Heather and Alison are grabbing snacks from the common room. They'll be back in a sec."

"Cool," I said. "You going riding soon?"

Julia stared at me for a looong time. "Are the non-riding clothes not a big enough hint?"

"Just asking," I said, my tone short like hers.

Brit took a breath and leaned forward on the couch, toward Julia.

"What are you and Trix working on?"

That was Brit. Always trying to stop fights before they started.

"What do you care?" Julia asked. She yanked her short hair into a ponytail. Pieces escaped around her face. "You're on the YENT. Like you want to know what advanced rider Julia is doing."

If Brit was fazed by Julia's comments, she didn't show it.

"We're friends," Brit said. "So I do care. But you don't have to tell me."

I didn't get Julia. After I'd helped prove that Jasmine had framed her and Alison, she'd at least made an effort not to openly hate me. But now, it was as if Brit and I had done something to her. She only really made an effort—and not always a great one—to be nice when Heather was around.

Before Julia could respond, the door opened and Heather and Alison walked in with two full trays of snacks and drinks.

"Hey!" Alison said, her greeting waaay more enthusiastic than Julia's.

Brit and I said hi to Heather and Alison as they set the trays on the dark-wood coffee table.

"Thanks for the snacks," I said.

Heather smoothed her black leggings and folded her arms. "Trust me," she said with the famous cocky-Heather look on her face. "I didn't drag Alison to the common room with me just to feed all your faces. You're going to need the caffeine and sugar, 'cause you'll be here as long as it takes to make my party plans perf."

"It's going to be amazing," I said. "Don't worry." Everyone else nodded.

That made Heather smile. She handed us all legal pads with purple paper and pens.

"You obvi want it to be *big*, right?" Alison asked. "I mean, a crazy-huge blowout where we invite everyone." She paused. "Well, by 'everyone,' I mean all the cool people we know."

Heather stared at her paper for a second. She blinked her mascara-coated lashes then looked up at all of us from her center spot on the couch.

"I was totally going to go that route, you know, like, the most luxurious party this school has ever seen. But . . ."

"But what?" Julia asked.

Heather gave her a look. "*But* that's what everyone expects. And I don't do what everyone thinks I'm going to do. I'm thinking a supertight invite-only party. Just us and a few other people. I mean, we really *don't* like too many other people."

Alison smiled. "So true. I love it! It's your birthday, so we're going to do whatever you want."

I sneaked a glance at Julia—her lips were pressed together and she wasn't saying a word. Julia wanted a huge party, I knew it. But she wasn't going to argue with Heather. Not when Heather already seemed kind of annoyed by her attitude lately.

Heather looked around at all of us, perfectly waxed eyebrows raised. "Start taking notes—hello."

We all looked down at our papers, waiting for her to continue.

"I want to throw it here," Heather said. "Something cozy—not anything where we have to get crazy dressed up. We'll make a small guest list, order food, and watch a ton of movies that we haven't had time to see lately."

Guests

Food

Movies

I wrote on my paper.

"That sounds perfect," Brit said. "I'd want a quiet party, too. I love the idea of watching movies. We could do a theater-themed party and transform the living room into a theater. We could have popcorn, M&M's—all the movie snacks."

Heather nodded, smiling. "I love that. And you guys pick out the movies. You know what I like. Or . . ." She eyed all of us. "I should *hope* you do."

"We'll get the list right," Alison said. She turned to a fresh sheet of paper, covering it with her hand as she wrote. "I've already got ideas."

Julia was the only one who hadn't said anything so far. I tried to send her an ESP message to say *something* before Heather jumped on her.

"That sounds fun," Julia said, almost as if she'd heard me yelling at her in my brain. But her enthusiastic tone sounded fake.

Heather turned her head toward Julia, her blond hair whipping around. She stared at Julia for a long time. Brit and I exchanged quick looks—both of us braced for a fight between the two of them. But Heather looked away from Julia and then back at us.

A tiny part of me felt sorry for Julia, but selfishly, I was glad it wasn't me. It had always made me feel worse when Heather ignored me and left me to worry about what she was going to do instead of attacking me. I wondered if Julia felt the same or if she was used to that kind of treatment by now.

"Let's talk food," I said.

And the five of us got into it and spent the next hour going back and forth about snacks and drinks. We decided on oversize soda cups, popcorn, lots of candy, and invites shaped like movie tickets.

"We should definitely have—" Heather stopped when her phone rang.

She picked up her BlackBerry, frowning when she saw the screen.

"My mother," she said to us, her tone matching her frown.

She pushed the call button and held the phone to her ear. "Hi, Mom," Heather said.

The rest of us looked back at our notepads, trying not to look as if we were listening to Heather's convo.

"Um, no, Mom, really," Heather said, her voice rising. "That's really generous of you and Dad, but my friends and I already started planning it and—"

Heather rubbed her forehead with one hand, listening. "Mom, I *know* turning thirteen is a big deal, but I—"

I could tell that Heather was struggling to keep her cool because if she fought back too much, Mrs. Fox wouldn't even listen to her. Kind of like she wasn't listening now.

"I've watched you plan so many amazing parties," Heather said. She took a huge breath, trying to keep her voice steady. "That's why I'm telling my friends exactly what to do. They understand just what I want—a low-key party in my suite."

Heather waved her free hand in the air, as if in defeat, and slumped backward. I could hear Mrs. Fox's voice though the phone. The cold voice seemed to suck some of the warmth out of the room.

Brit and I looked at each other, sending *this sounds bad* signals with our eyes.

"Okay, Mom," Heather said. Her voice was quiet. "Thank you." She moved the phone from her ear, holding down the end call button until the orange AT&T screen flashed and the phone went dark.

Everyone looked at her, but no one spoke. Alison, Julia, Brit, and I were waiting for Heather to speak first.

Heather ran her fingers through her hair and tossed her notebook on the coffee table, almost knocking over Alison's Sprite.

"My mother will be here on Wednesday," Heather said.

"*What?*" all of us said in unison.

Heather didn't even look furious—just resigned. "Apparently, she's been planning my party for months, and it's not going to be something we throw. She's wants it to be the social event of the fall."

"And she's *coming*?" Alison asked. "Why? She never visits school."

Heather's laugh was bitter. "Right? But of course she has to oversee my party to make sure everything is Fox-worthy."

"There's no talking her out of it?" Brit asked.

"You don't know my mother," Heather said. "No one dissuades her from anything once she's made up her mind. She's already talked to the headmistress. She's going to be here early Wednesday afternoon to oversee the caterer, *and* the party planner that she hired to basically micromanage every aspect of the party."

"She wouldn't even consider letting you plan your own?" Alison asked. She shook her head. "I know your mom, but this is so unfair. It's your *thirteenth* birthday. Maybe you can call her back later and try to explain again."

Heather shook her head. "She won't listen, Alison. You know that." Heather stared with a blank look for a few seconds. "Instead of movie night, she already planned a fancy party that would be a big deal even for the Waldorf."

Julia sat up straighter, her eyes wide. "Details, puh-lease!"

"Oh, it's the usual Fox type of party. Expensive dresses for the girls, black tie for the guys, a transformed ballroom, caviar, and other food that no one will eat." Heather sighed. "Add to that my mom, who will be in a ridic frenzy."

"I know how your mom is," I said. "And you're right, there's no talking her out of *anything*. So, we'll go along with her party, but that doesn't mean we won't have fun."

Heather nodded, getting up off the couch. "Duh. Be right back." She walked away toward her room, her shoulders slumped a little.

"We'll go to her mom's party," Alison whispered. "But we *have* to throw her the party she wants."

"A surprise party sounds perfect!" Brit said.

The rest of us nodded, stopping the second we heard Heather's footsteps. With the four of us playing party planners, I had no doubt Heather's thirteenth birthday was going to be better than she could ever imagine.

4
TABLE FOR TWO

I HELD UP A ROYAL BLUE CARDIGAN, A WHITE v-neck tee and skinny jeans. "Date-approved?" I asked Brit.

Brit eyed my clothing choices, nodding. "So approved. With your ankle boots?"

"Love."

I'd just finished going through my closet, looking for the right outfit for my Sweet Shoppe date with Jacob. I changed, then sat at my desk chair to apply makeup.

"Are you still getting, like, a dozen texts or e-mails a day from guys wanting to go out with you?" I asked Brit.

She blushed. "Please. I've had a couple of guys ask me out, but none I've wanted to date. There just hasn't been that spark—like with you and Jacob."

"You haven't been here too long," I said. "I know you'll find someone—when you're ready. You'll meet the right guy."

Brit put down her phone. "I *might* have met *someone*."

"What?" I almost dropped my foundation brush. "Who?"

"I was talking to Andy after a lesson," Brit said. "And he's so sweet and cute and funny."

"Omigod! Andy would be perfect for you!"

I couldn't believe I hadn't thought of the two of them together before. Andy, an intermediate rider, was one of my friends at the stable.

Brit smiled. "He's so gorgeous. I mean, I don't even know if he likes me since he hasn't asked me out or anything, but we've talked a few times. I *think* he might like me."

"Andy would be dumb if he didn't," I said. "He's a really nice guy, Brit. If he wants to go out with you, definitely go."

"Hopefully, we'll keep talking and he'll ask me," Brit said. She sat up on her bed.

"He will," I said, dabbing concealer on my chin. "It's so exciting that you have a crush!"

We both giggled, and I told Brit everything I knew

about Andy—that he was smart, funny, a good rider, and he had pizza at least three times a week. I stopped talking when my phone buzzed.

I opened a new e-mail and saw a Google alert that made me clench my Dior lip gloss—one I only used on special occasions.

"What's wrong?" Brit asked.

I got up without answering her and opened my computer. I motioned her over on my bed, and she watched as I opened Firefox and clicked on a bookmark.

"Oh, no," Brit said.

We both looked at the screen—staring at the Canterwood gossip blog. The entry was short, but it didn't need to be longer to cause more damage.

Rumor has it that a certain soon-to-be teen queen is having a birthday bash that'll be the blowout of the century. If only all of her lowly worker bees were so happy about the special date. One, for example, would love to see this birthday blow.

"Heather's party," Brit and I said together.

We read the entry again to ourselves.

"Heather's mom *just* called her," Brit said.

I closed my laptop lid in disgust. "I know. How did it get around school so fast? Unless the Trio already started telling people."

"But who is the blogger talking about?" Brit asked. "We haven't talked to anyone, and Julia *and* Alison want Heather's public party to be awesome."

I shrugged. "I have no clue. It seems like the blogger is talking about Julia, Alison, you, or me, but you're right—none of us want Heather to have a bad birthday."

Brit shook her head. "I hate this. This post is obviously a lie, but it's going to start making things crazy if people believe the blogger."

I pulled on my cardigan and put my phone in my black purse. "You're right. But, so far, the blogger has zero credibility. Everyone seems more fascinated by the posts than gullible enough to believe them."

"Let's hope it stays that way," Brit said.

She waved me out as I headed down Orchard's hallway to The Sweet Shoppe. I rifled through my purse, already feeling the need to re-gloss, when familiar laughter made me look up.

Callie Harper.

And Paige Parker.

My two ex—best friends.

Both girls looked away from each other and stopped laughing. They were carrying an armload of textbooks. Paige's long red-gold hair looked pretty in loose waves, and Callie's black hair was pulled back in a French braid. Orchard was Callie's dorm, too. Paige must have come over to study with Callie.

I paused midstep, then kept walking. We passed each other in the hallway and neither girl said a word. Callie's dark brown eyes and Paige's green ones stared straight ahead—not looking at me.

I pushed open the side exit door with my palms on the glass instead of the handle. I couldn't get out of Orchard fast enough. Light from the campus lanterns made warm yellow shadows over me as I hurried down the sidewalk.

The last thing I wanted to think about before meeting Jacob was Callie and Paige, but I couldn't stop my thoughts from going there.

Paige had been my BFF and roommate before I'd moved in with Brit. She was also friends with Callie, my other ex-BFF. I'd lost Callie over Jacob. Then, Paige had backstabbed me by siding with Callie.

I'd gotten used to the emptiness of not having Callie in my life, but the loss of Paige still hurt. More than anything, I wanted our friendship back. Paige had been there with me through everything and, even though I had a new friendship with Brit, it didn't stop me from missing Paige.

I shook myself out of my memory and realized The Sweet Shoppe was just ahead. I didn't want my time with Jacob to be ruined, so I shook Paige and Callie out of my brain.

Scents of fall treats—pumpkin spice–flavored coffee, apple tarts, and hazelnut cookies—drifted out of the cozy shop, as students came in and out. I walked under the blue and white awning and up the stairs to the building. Inside, I looked around.

I didn't have to look far.

At a table for two near the back, Jacob caught my gaze. His hazel eyes settled on mine and his smile made thoughts of Callie and Paige disappear. He had that effect on me.

"Hi, Sash," Jacob said.

"Hi." I walked over to him, grinning.

I stopped in front of him and he took my hands, gently pulling me close to him. I squeezed his hands to try and keep myself steady. Our lips brushed together and his breath, minty and sweet, was gentle on my face when we parted.

"Hi," I said again like an idiot.

"You look amazing," Jacob said, pulling out my chair.

I sat down and gazed across the table at him. Our

being together was still so new—I almost couldn't believe it. Being out in public with him made me feel giddy and self-conscious at the same time. I couldn't help but wonder if girls looked at me and wondered why *beyond* hot and popular Jacob Schwartz was dating Sasha Silver.

"Thanks," I said. "So do you."

And he did look great. His light brown hair was messy—in that on-purpose way—and his slightly faded tan made his teeth look superwhite.

"I might have had *some* kind of idea what you like," Jacob said, his tone teasing. "So, I ordered two hot chocolates that should be here any sec."

"Yum. Perfect," I said.

As if on cue, a waitress walked over with a tray carrying two steaming white and blue striped mugs of hot chocolate. She placed a bowl of mini-marshmallows and two spoons in between us.

"Enjoy," she said, walking back to the counter.

I looked at the marshmallows, smiling without being able to stop. I'd met Jacob here once, long before we'd been torn apart by Heather, and we'd had hot chocolate. Jacob had noticed I'd eaten all my marshmallows and had spooned some from his cup into mine.

We put marshmallows into our mugs and took sips.

"This was such a great choice," I said. "I guess you *do* know that I sort of like chocolate. Just a little."

Jacob laughed. "Yeah, only a tiny bit."

His gaze made me feel warmer than the hot chocolate on my tongue.

"How's your weekend so far?" Jacob asked, stirring his drink.

"Busy and . . ." I trailed off, not wanting to talk about stuff that would bring down the mood.

"And what?" Jacob asked, his tone gentle. His eyes went back and forth across my face. "I can tell something's up. What's going on?"

I sighed, looking up at him from my mug. He knew me too well. "Today's just been a little stressful. At the Trio's, we were planning Heather's party and her mom called."

"Uh-oh," Jacob said. I'd given him a brief history of Mrs. Fox before.

"Yeah, giant uh-oh. She'd already planned Heather's entire party as the exact opposite of what Heather wanted. She's coming to school and it's going to make Heather freak."

"Lame," Jacob said. "You know I'm not Heather's

biggest fan, but you guys have sort of a friendship now. And anyway, she should get the birthday she wants."

"I know. I agree, and so do Julia, Alison, and Brit. We're still giving Heather the party she wants—it's going to be a surprise party after her mom's *event*."

Jacob reached over, running his thumb across the top of my hand. "That's what I love about you. You're insanely busy, but you're taking time to help throw a surprise party for someone you used to not be able to even be in the same room with."

It was almost as if his finger had burned my skin where he'd touched me.

"Heather deserves it," I said. "And you're right—we used to hate each other and we both made lots of mistakes. But it wasn't worth it after a while. It took too much energy to keep attacking each other."

"You never stop impressing me," Jacob said.

His words repeated on a loop in my head for seconds before I was able to respond.

"That means a lot," I said. "I just hope Heather and I can keep our relationship civil like it has been. Things are crazy enough at school without having that drama."

I took a sip of hot chocolate and melted marshmallows.

"What else is going on?" Jacob asked. "You looked a little rattled when you walked in."

I picked a marshmallow out of the bowl, tossing it into my mouth.

"I don't want to keep talking about me."

Jacob, following my lead, put a few marshmallows in his mouth. "You don't have to talk about anything, but I want you to know you can."

"I know you're there to listen," I said. "And thank you. I always know I can talk to you."

"Anytime," Jacob said. I wanted to hug him again— he looked so touchable in his black waffle-knit shirt.

"I just saw Callie and Paige on the way out," I said. "I know there's zero chance Callie and I will ever be friends again, but I can't stop hoping Paige and I will work things out."

"I know you miss Paige," Jacob said. "She was your best friend. I'm sure she feels the same way. If you both want to fix your friendship, it'll happen."

And, somehow, I believed him.

"I hope so. I just know it's going to take time."

Jacob, showing every bit of the guy I'd been drawn to, listened and offered his opinion about the Paige situation while we ordered and consumed slices of pumpkin pie with whipped cream.

"It's all going to work out," Jacob said. "Promise."

He reached across the table with his spoon, gently tapping a bit of whipped cream onto the top of my nose.

I laughed and dodged his second attempt. "Jacob!"

Still giggling, I wiped off the cream. Jacob watched, a raised eyebrow paired with a half smile.

I shook my head at him, pretending to be mad. "Sooo mature," I teased.

Jacob pretended to tip an imaginary hat. "Always."

I looked down at the crumbs on my plate, not wanting to leave Jacob yet.

"Do you have to be back at Orchard yet?" Jacob asked, his own plate and mug empty.

"Nope. What about you? Are you going to Blackwell now?" Jacob's dorm was on the other side of campus.

Jacob checked the time on his phone. "I don't have to be back yet. If you want . . . we could do something else."

"I'd love that," I said. "Video games at the media center?"

That made Jacob smile. "Yeah, I wouldn't enjoy that at all," he teased. "Video games and you."

I smiled back. "C'mon then. We haven't played in *forever*. But that doesn't mean I'm not going to win."

Jacob stood, putting a tip on the table. "Oh, Sasha. I think the sugar messed with your brain."

"Excuse *you*?" I bantered back.

"Just because I like you doesn't mean I'm going to let you win," Jacob said.

"*Let* me win?" I pretend-rolled my eyes. "Maybe I've been practicing in the media center, like, all the time."

I could feel Jacob staring at me while I picked up my purse. We walked out of The Sweet Shoppe, laughing.

We walked along the sidewalk, the streetlights providing just enough light so I could see Jacob's features. He took my hand in his and we walked together—silent— as we took in the crisp Connecticut air and clear sky. Thousands of diamondlike stars lit up the dark, and I held Jacob's hand tighter.

"I missed you," I said, my breath visible.

"I missed you," Jacob said. He glanced over at me. "I hate that things happened the way they did, but I wouldn't change anything about us getting together— then or now."

"Me neither."

Jacob nodded. "I just . . . knew what it felt like to be

so close to being your boyfriend. Then, to be with someone else and have to watch you with another guy . . . I'm just so glad to have this chance with you."

"I'm scared sometimes," I admitted. "It's so perfect; I'm afraid I'll do something to mess it up."

Jacob stopped on the sidewalk, turning to me. "You *never* have to be afraid when you're with me, okay?" He brushed my cheek with his thumb.

"Okay." The word came out so quiet, I almost wasn't sure if he heard me.

But Jacob smiled and started toward the media canter, tugging my hand. "C'mon, player. You've talked a big game."

"You're so on."

We reached the media center and walked inside. The massive center housed a giant movie theater, multiple gaming and screening rooms, dozens of flat-screen TVs, and DVD and video game collections in the thousands.

"Let's go find an empty room," Jacob said.

Hand in hand, we passed the theater entrance.

"We spent a lot of time in there," I said.

"Mr. Ramirez's film class last year was the best. I never would have watched half the movies he got us to see if they hadn't been part of the class."

"Me too. But I'm glad I did."

We headed for a room in the back and turned down a long hallway.

"Hey!"

Jacob and I looked up to see Andy.

"Hi!" We both said.

"Are you guys on a daaate?" Andy asked.

I pretended to glare at him. "Yes. But now we're here to chill and play video games."

A look passed between Jacob and me. I knew him well enough to know it was cool to invite Andy to play.

"Want to join?" I asked Andy. "Jacob and I have been trash talking each other about who's going down. Jacob, because he's scaaared, wants a partner. He's too nervous to take me on." I looked pointedly at Jacob.

Jacob gave me the same look back. "Don't listen to her," he said to Andy. "She's the one who needs backup." He folded his arms and looked at me. "Got anyone in mind?"

It clicked in my brain.

Andy.

Brit.

"I'll be right back," I told the boys.

I walked away from them and pulled my BlackBerry out of my pocket.

Sasha Silver:

OMG, u have 2 get 2 the media cntr right now!!

It took Brit only half a minute to start typing back.

Brit Chan:

Ummm . . . why?

Sasha Silver:

Because ANDY's here. Jacob and I finished r date and r play-ing video games w/him.

Brit Chan:

Noooo way am I just showing up like some lame person you set up for Andy!

Sasha Silver:

It's not like that at all—swear. It's boys vs. girls. I need a partner, so it only makes sense that I asked u.

Brit Chan:

Ohhh . . .

Sasha Silver:

It's only a *bonus* that you get to hang w/Andy and c if u rlly rlly like him. :D

Brit Chan:

LOL. K. BRT.

I exited out of BBM, grinning.

I walked back to the guys who were already in a debate about what we were going to play.

"Brit's on her way," I said. "Together, we're going to make you both cry."

Andy and Jacob laughed, but not in a mean way.

"Sorry, but no way," Andy said. "But, uh, Brit's coming?" He ran a hand over his dark hair.

"Yeah," I said, trying to sound casual. "You guys know each other from the stable, so I thought it would be cool."

Andy nodded so hard, I thought his head would fly off. "Yeah, um, definitely. It's cool. Very cool. I'm glad you asked her. That's cool."

I hid my smile at how many times he'd just said "cool." He *so* like-liked Brit—it was obvious.

We talked about what room we wanted while we waited for Brit. And, ten minutes later, Brit walked over to us.

She'd changed into black skinny jeans, ankle boots with tiny silver buckles, and a teal v-neck sweater. Casual, but I knew she'd agonized over what to wear. But the boys would never know that Brit had likely sweated over every piece of clothing.

"Hi," Brit said. She smiled and Andy was the last person she looked at. Her eyelashes fluttered a little when she looked at him before her gaze darted to me.

"Hey," I said, walking over to her side. "I'm happy you weren't busy. Let's go find an empty room."

Andy, Brit, Jacob, and I walked through the center of the large room and took a left down one of the hallways. Brit and Andy, ahead of Jacob and me, were walking a little far apart. We passed a few rooms that already had students either watching movies or playing PlayStation.

"Found one," Jacob said.

I followed him into the room, and Andy stepped back to let Brit walk inside before him. They both eyed the big tan couch. Brit sat near the left arm and, with a quick wink to her, I left a space between us when I sat down. The boys set up the Nintendo system and we all agreed to play Super Smash Bros. Melee. I knew it was Jacob's fave.

Andy turned, pausing for a second, when he saw the open seats. He could either sit next to Brit or me. Jacob, hanging back and untangling a controller cord, let Andy make the decision.

And he made the right one.

Andy walked over and sat next to Brit. The two smiled at each other, and Brit couldn't stop smiling as Jacob handed all of us controllers.

"We've got to beat them," I said, leaning over Andy to talk to Brit.

"Given," she said. She giggled when she looked at Andy. "Sorry. But you're going down."

"Not a chance," Jacob said, teasingly.

We all chose our characters and started to battle. Unfortunately for Brit and me, "battle" wasn't exactly what we were doing. Jacob had taught me how to play and Brit had played before, but we couldn't hold up against Jacob and Andy.

It got to the level of . . . embarrassing.

"Did you guys rig this?" Brit asked.

"Sorry," Andy laughed. "Want to play something else?"

"No way!" Brit and I said in unison.

We started a new round and, somehow, Brit and I started scoring points.

"Ha!" Brit teased. "Andy, my grandmother could have done better than that."

Andy faked trash talking right back. The two of them kept going at each other, laughing harder and harder at who came up with the more creative insult.

I glanced at Jacob a few times and we shared a look— both of us sensed the obvious chemistry between Brit and Andy.

All too soon, the media center started to close down and it was time for us to head back to our dorms.

We walked outside together, everyone happy from having fun.

"I *still* think Sasha and I won the most rounds," Brit said. "Andy, your mental scorecard must have malfunctioned."

Andy mock-rolled his eyes. "Fiiine. Next time, you keep score."

The four of us stopped a few steps away from the media center, standing under one of the streetlamps.

"See you later," I said to Jacob. He squeezed my hand, and I could see his beautiful green eyes even in the dim light.

"Bye, Sash."

"Brit," Andy started. "I really had fun with you tonight. Maybe we could go to The Sweet Shoppe or something soon? If you want."

Brit's smile said it all. "That would be great. Do you have your phone?"

Andy pulled out a sleek black phone and handed it to her. Brit punched in her number and gave it to him.

"Text me whenever," she said.

I cheered in my head. This couldn't have gone better!

I'd had an *amazing* time with Jacob, and Brit and Andy were definitely going on a date soon. Andy was the perfect guy, for Brit and I could barely stop myself from hugging her with excitement.

"See you guys later," I said.

"Bye," Jacob and Andy said.

Brit and I started down the sidewalk toward Orchard and the guys headed for Blackwell.

"Omigod!" Brit said. She grabbed my arm so tight she almost cut off my circulation.

"I know!" I said. "You're going on a date with Andy. He *definitely* like-likes you! And now you know for sure. But, I've got to say, I told you that he liked you."

Brit almost skipped. "He does! I mean, we had fun this one time, but things felt so good. I'm more excited than nervous to go on a date with him to The Sweet Shoppe."

"You definitely have no reason to be nervous," I said. "You know him a lot better after tonight."

Brit and I linked arms and for the rest of the walk back, analyzing every second of the night.

5

CALLIE VS BRIT

I WAS UP BEFORE SIX SUNDAY MORNING.
Mr. Conner had scheduled a special practice because of
the upcoming Huntington Classic. Bleary-eyed, Brit and
I were in our horses' stalls by six-thirty.

Charm snoozed on and off as I groomed him. He'd
been in his warm stall all night and not in the pasture,
so he just needed a light brushing. I swept the body
brush over him, picked his hooves, combed his mane
and tail, and he was ready to be tacked up.

In the tack room, I almost bumped into Heather.
Unlike me, her hair was perfectly straight, she looked
wide awake and had even done her makeup.

I shook my head. "How?"

"What?" she asked, turning with Aristocrat's saddle over her arm.

"It's not even seven and you look like you've been up for hours."

"Some people don't sleep all day," Heather said, tossing a grin over her shoulder. "See you in the arena."

She left me alone to gather Charm's tack. I slung his bridle over my shoulder and put his pad and saddle over my right arm.

It didn't take long to tack him up, and we headed for the heated indoor arena. I was glad Mr. Conner wasn't making us practice outside in the cold morning air. Charm wouldn't have minded, though. His coat was getting wooly.

I walked Charm down the aisle and stopped him just inside the indoor arena. I stuck my foot into the stirrup and swung myself into the saddle. When I saw the dressage markers along the wall, my stomach tightened a little. Charm and I needed more work on dressage, and I was glad Mr. Conner was making us practice, but I wished I'd worked more on my own first. Brit and Callie were the best dressage riders on our team. It made me feel a little insecure to do dressage in front of them.

Just remember the trick Kim taught you, I told myself, thinking back to early dressage sessions at Briar Creek, my first stable. I looked at the dressage markers—*A, K, E, H, C, M, B, F. All King Edward's horses can make big fences.* I repeated that twice to myself. If I was ever going to be a good rider and have a shot at making the United States Equestrian team, I *had* to get better at dressage.

Brit, Callie, and Heather were already warming up their horses. Charm and I joined the others trotting along the wall. Charm, frisky this morning, bobbed his head and tried to stretch his neck. I gave him more rein, letting him move a little more freely as we started at a walk. I moved Charm along the wall, letting him fall into line behind Callie and Black Jack.

I tried to focus on Charm, but couldn't help but watch Callie and Jack. Callie had never stopped practicing hard, but she had stepped up her game even more since she'd made the YENT. She sat to Jack's trot which was smoother than I'd ever seen. I yanked my gaze away from her when Mr. Conner stepped into the arena.

He stopped in the center of the arena, his ever-present clipboard under his arm. Mr. Conner held up a hand, signaling for us to stop.

Callie, Brit, Heather, and I slowed our horses in front

of him. Charm and I went between Brit and Heather. Charm eyed Aristocrat and the beautiful darker chestnut gelding stared straight ahead. On our other side, Apollo didn't look nervous at all. He stood relaxed—one ear forward and one back.

"Morning, everyone," Mr. Conner said, tapping a boot against the dirt floor. "As you can see by the markers, we'll be working on dressage this morning. It was necessary to hold a Sunday practice since we want to be at our best for Huntington. We will *not*, however, over-practice."

That was always something Mr. Conner drilled into us. Even though we were YENT riders and he wanted us to do well, he never allowed us to push our horses or ourselves too hard. That's something Jasmine had tried to pull during her short time at Canterwood, and it hadn't gone over well with Mr. Conner.

At. All.

"We're going to do a few exercises and then we'll run though the dressage test I e-mailed all of you last week," Mr. Conner said. "You've had ample time to memorize it, so I will *not* be calling out any instructions unless you get lost during your test."

I'd done dressage tests without a caller before, but

not with Callie, Brit, *and* Heather watching. I tried to push away the nerves—determined not to allow them to affect Charm. He was in tune with my body and he'd know if I was scared.

Mr. Conner gave us a reassuring smile. "Let's all spread out in the arena, and we'll get started."

The four of us turned our horses and headed for separate corners of the arena. Again, I glanced at Callie. Her black breeches, boots, and crisp white shirt were spotless. She looked dressed for Huntington.

"We're going to start with spirals," Mr. Conner called out. "Pay attention to how loose or tight your horses' muscles feel as they move through the exercise. Do two spirals in both directions at a walk, then try it at a trot."

I squeezed my boots against Charm's sides and let him walk a few strides in a straight line before pulling on the right rein to ease him into a circle. I kept my eyes between Charm's ears and sank my weight into the saddle. Charm responded by starting to circle and I kept my attention on him.

Our spirals got tighter and Charm's body bent easily though the exercise. *Good boy,* I said to Charm in my head. He was *so* getting carrots after this.

We reversed directions and did the spiral at a walk in the opposite direction.

"Looking great, everyone," Mr. Conner said. "Keep it up."

I couldn't help but smile at the praise.

Charm felt loose beneath me and when his body curled into the final round of the spiral, I let him straighten.

"Nice," I whispered to him.

Now it was time to try a trot.

I glanced over, seeing Brit and Apollo trotting through their spiral. They were circling between the *K* and *A* markers. Apollo's gray coat looked like shiny steel under the arena lights.

Charm and I turned, ready to start the spiral at a trot, and I saw Callie. She and Jack were also trotting though their spiral, but Callie's attention wasn't on Jack—it was on Brit. Jack, following the direction of Callie's gaze, trotted just to the side and stepped out of his once near-perfect spiral.

"Callie, pay attention, please," Mr. Conner said. "Jack lost his focus because you did."

Callie ducked her head and refocused her attention on Jack. Before Charm and I made a mistake, too, I stopped watching everyone else.

We completed the spirals and rode back to the center of the arena for more instructions.

"Good work, everyone," Mr. Conner said. "I would like to see all of you pay more attention to your own horses instead of each other."

Beside me, Callie seemed to shrink lower into her saddle.

"At Huntington, there will be many riders that you'll want to watch," Mr. Conner continued, looking up from his clipboard. "If you're already eyeing your own team-mates, you're going to have trouble not watching your competition. This is something you all need to work on to avoid problems in the future."

We all nodded.

"Now, you're each going to try the dressage test," Mr. Conner said. He moved away from the center of the arena and toward the wall. "Sasha, you're up first."

Greaaat.

I was half scared and half relieved to get my turn over first. Callie, Brit, and Heather walked their horses to the wall and out of the way of the markers. I let Charm follow them since we had to ride back to the center of the arena as part of the test. It wasn't long or too complicated, but it felt daunting from the saddle.

After one breath, I made myself tell Charm to trot to

the center of the arena and stop at the *X* marker. Charm stood still until I saluted and asked him to move at a sitting trot toward *C*. Charm had good energy and moved well beneath me.

We made a twenty-meter circle, then went straight along the wall at a posting trot. At *H*, we made a sharp turn and crossed the arena to *M*. At *M*, we made another circle and I turned Charm out of the circle as we headed for *B* at a slow, steady canter. We passed *B* and at *F*, I eased Charm to a trot, then a walk. We made our final circle, walked by *A*, and I sat to Charm's trot as we headed for *X*—our last marker.

This was one of the best tests we'd ever done! *But don't mess it up now,* I told myself. Charm's trot stayed steady, and he didn't try to rush like he did sometimes when we got close to the end of a test.

At *X*, I drew Charm to a smooth halt. I saluted sharply and felt like I could breathe again. I turned Charm back to face Heather, Brit, Callie, and Mr. Conner. I patted Charm's neck.

"You were *great*," I whispered.

I stopped Charm next to Heather.

"Not too bad," she said, loud enough so only I could hear her.

I knew Charm and I did well if *Heather* was giving us props.

"Excellent ride, Sasha," Mr. Conner said. He smiled at me and stopped in front of Charm to look up at me. "Your circles were well-proportioned and Charm was alert during each movement. Keep your diagonal lines a little straighter next time, but that was a great test."

"Thank you," I said.

I rubbed Charm's shoulder before sitting back in the saddle, relaxed and glad my turn was done.

"Brit, you may ride next," Mr. Conner said.

Brit gathered Apollo's reins and began the test. Throughout her ride, I kept sneaking glances at Callie. Her eyes were narrowed on Brit. Callie was used to being the star dressage rider on our team.

Until Brit.

Brit did each movement of the test with precision that I'd only seen on TV. Even though I wasn't even close to an expert in dressage, I'd watched enough riders perform tests that didn't even compare to Brit's. Callie's lips, pressed together, were obvious signals that she was nervous. Even though we weren't best friends anymore, I knew her too well. Callie was intimidated by Brit.

It was going to make her fight that much harder to win.

Brit finished her test and Mr. Conner smiled at her. "Well done," he said. "You and Apollo are in tune and performed exactly as I hoped you would. Thank you."

Not even a hint of cockiness from Mr. Conner's words appeared on Brit's face. She let Apollo back beside Charm, and I held my hand low for a quiet high five. Brit gave me a quick smile before we focused on Mr. Conner again.

"Callie, if you're ready," Mr. Conner said. "You may start."

Callie didn't waste a second. She moved Black Jack forward with a seamless movement and the pair started the dressage test. Every movement was fluid from marker to marker. I wanted to glance at Brit and Heather, to see if they were as impressed as I was, but I couldn't look away from the performance. Every curve, circle, and transition Jack made looked like part of a dance.

Where is this *coming from?* I wondered. I'd seen Callie ride dressage a zillion times and she'd always been brilliant, but nothing like this.

When Callie halted Jack at X, I leaned over to Heather. "What. Was. That?" I whispered.

Heather turned her head, staring at me from under the brim of her helmet. "The start of a dressage war."

6

DID YOU
MISS ME?

"YOU REALLY HAVE TO GIVE ME, LIKE, A private lesson sometime," I told Brit. We walked back from the stable after our dressage lesson.

"Oh, please," Brit said. "You definitely don't need any help from *me*. But if you want to practice together that would be fun."

"Def." I paused, thinking about the lesson as we walked up the sidewalk toward Orchard. Callie and Brit's rides had been amazing, then Heather had given a performance that I was sure had made me—not Charm—look like I belonged on the beginner team.

"I keep saying I'm going to work harder on dressage and I hardly ever do," I said. "I love flatwork and jumping so much. And so does Charm! But we've got to be better rounded for Huntington."

Brit stuck her hands in her jacket pockets. "We all have to be at the top of our game for this show. It's going to set the tone for the entire season."

"Yeah, and—" I stopped midsentence when my phone buzzed in my pocket. I grabbed my BlackBerry and saw I had a new text. Maybe it was Jacob . . .

I opened the message and saw a name I'd never wanted to see again.

Ever.

To: Sasha Silver

From: Jasmine King

Long time no talk! Did u miss me? U won't have 2 4 much longer! I'll c u and ur apparently new BFF Heather @ Huntington. Can't wait! xx

"Ugh," I said, moaning.

"What's wrong?" Brit asked.

I handed her my phone, not saying a word. Brit took it and scanned the message. She handed it back to me, shaking her head.

"*I* can't wait to finally meet the infamous Jasmine King," Brit said. "This is perfect, Sash. She's going into Huntington thinking she's already making you uncomfortable and you know she sent a similar message to Heather and Callie."

"That's her style," I grumbled.

"So she's going to think you'll all be freaked out about seeing her and that it'll rattle you enough to give her and Wellington an edge. Guess what?"

"What?" I eyed Brit warily.

"She's *totally* wrong."

"We do have a great team," I said. "But you don't know this girl. She's vicious. She'll do anything to win— even at the cost of her horse. I've seen it. Jasmine is the most ruthless rider I've ever seen, and she's not going to lose without a fight."

Brit didn't look worried. "Then we'll fight. You just said you want to practice dressage more. Now you have an even bigger incentive."

"I definitely do."

We were quiet the rest of the short walk back to Orchard. Inside the front hall, Stephanie, the dorm monitor, was putting up fall decorations. She stood in front of one of the hall tables and put vanilla frosting– scented Yankee candles in a pretty pattern surrounded by real-looking red, orange, and yellow leaves.

Usually, I'd get excited about decorations of any kind

and would want to immediately add festive touches to my room. But right now, the only thing I could think about was the text from Jasmine.

Inside our room, I pulled off my boots and flopped onto my bed. Brit went to shower and I opened Jasmine's text again. I hit forward, typed in Heather's name and wrote *what do u think?* above the text.

Seconds later, my phone vibrated. I opened the message, sure that Heather would have a snarky response to Jas's text that would make me feel better.

To: Sasha Silver

From: Heather Fox

That we better b ready 4 a showdown.

7
PASSING NOTES

IN MONDAY MORNING'S ENGLISH CLASS, I was scribbling down answers to questions from Mr. Davidson's homework that I hadn't finished Sunday night. I'd been too tired after my lesson and the rest of my homework had kept me at my desk until I'd fallen asleep.

I filled in the last blank and shoved the now-finished worksheet back in my pink folder, glad to not have any late homework, especially not in this advanced class. I'd been the only one in the room for a while because I'd gotten there early. I looked up when the doorknob turned.

Paige stepped inside, giving me a tiny smile when she saw me.

"Um, hi," she said.

"Hey."

There wasn't any venom in our tones—they sounded the same. Sad and tired.

Paige was wearing a cranberry-colored three-quarters sleeve shirt that I'd never seen before, with over-the-knee black boots and jeans. I wondered if she'd gone shopping with Geena, her new roommate. Even after all this time, thinking about it was still hard to digest. I opened my folder, shuffling papers, and pretending there was something interesting in it.

"Can we talk for a sec?" Paige asked. She sat beside me, placing her leather messenger bag on the floor.

I glanced at her, unsure if I'd heard her right. "Of course," I said. I had no clue what this was about. Paige and I weren't enemies anymore, and our relationship had never been *exactly* that, even after the Callie thing, but we'd been sort of frozen and hadn't moved forward to repairing our past friendship.

Our past BFF-ness.

And it still hurt.

Paige's green eyes focused on mine. She took a deep breath and twisted a lock of red-gold hair around her finger. I shifted in my seat, hating the discomfort between us.

"Sasha, I wanted to know—"

Paige closed her mouth when the door to the classroom burst open with such force that we both jumped. Vanessa, a girl in our class, walked inside laughing with Alison. Behind them came a few other students and Mr. Davidson.

I looked at Paige, desperate to know what she'd wanted. But it was obviously something Paige didn't want to discuss in front of everyone. She gave me a *sorry* look and opened her notebook.

Mr. Davidson went to his desk and started taking attendance.

I'm going to have to sit through this entire class and be tortured, I thought. I'd have to wait until the end to see if Paige wanted to finish what she'd started saying. What if she said nothing at all—like it had never happened?

I felt something being pressed into my hand. I looked down, under the table, and a tiny folded up piece of paper was in my hand. On the ripped up piece of notebook paper, in purple pen, was a note in Paige's handwriting.

Can we meet up and talk? Pls?

For a long minute, I stared at the note, reading Paige's familiar handwriting over and over.

I finally wrote back.

2mrw?

Paige read my note and handed me another.

Absolutely. Text me whenever.

For the rest of English class, I tried to focus on the lesson and not think about whatever Paige wanted to talk to me about. I wasn't too nervous—the way we'd just talked hadn't been contentious. Paige didn't seem like she was asking to meet with me just to fight. Or, at least, I hoped not.

Later that afternoon, I was heading to free period when I saw Eric looking at a handout from one of his classes.

"Hey," I said, walking up to him.

He looked up smiled. "Hey, Sasha. How's everything?"

"Good," I said. "Busy, obviously. But good."

He adjusted the math textbook and notebook in his hand. "I'm glad. I'm happy you're doing okay."

"Actually, I'm doing more than okay," I said, my tone soft. "And it's partly because of you."

Eric leaned his shoulder back against the wall, looking at me with his intense dark eyes. "What did *I* do?"

"What you did with Jacob—the riding lessons—I can't thank you enough. That was the best Halloween surprise ever. I knew you were my friend, but what you did was beyond amazing." I swallowed. "It couldn't have been easy for you to be around Jacob. You did it because we're friends, and I really, *really* appreciate it."

Eric looked at me with soft eyes. "It was kind of awkward at times, sure. But Jacob cares about you and when he asked me, there was no way I would have said no. We *are* friends, Sash."

I watched. Standing there in his navy T-shirt and jeans, Eric looked like a guy I was lucky to have as my friend.

"I'm so happy we're able to be friends. We should definitely hang out sometime, if you want."

Eric nodded. "Definitely. I'm sure you're going to be practicing like crazy for Huntington. We could work in the arena sometime, if you want."

"You're on. I'd like that."

We both smiled at each other.

"See you later," Eric said. "I've got to get to class."

"Bye."

I felt good as we split up in the hallway. I headed to free period and sat in the back, so I could BBM Jacob before I started homework. Keeping one eye on Ms. Utz, who was monitoring this free period, I took out my phone.

Sasha Silver:

Just wanted 2 tell u that I talked 2 Eric a sec ago.

I got a few questions on my English worksheet answered before I felt my phone vibrate.

Jacob Schwartz:

Oh, yeah?

Sasha Silver:

I saw him and wanted 2 thank him for giving u riding lessons.

Jacob Schwartz:

That was cool of u. I'm glad u guys r friends.

As if it wasn't already official, I had THE best boyfriend.

Sasha Silver:

Me too. I'm glad you're cool w/it. We're going 2 practice 2gether sometime since I have lots of work 4 Huntington.

Jacob Schwartz:

That's a good idea. Prob will make u less nervous since he's not your competition like Heather or even Brit.

Sasha Silver:

Yeah, I think so too. I don't feel competitive w/Brit or H, but it'll def b a nice break to

"Sasha? Do you not have enough homework to keep you busy?"

I yanked my head up, and Ms. Utz was standing over me, her arms crossed.

"No, I mean, yes," I said, flustered. "Sorry."

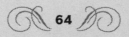

Ms. Utz held out an open hand. "I'll hold onto your phone until the period is over."

Blushing, I handed her my BlackBerry.

After a stern look, she turned away and walked up the aisle to the front of the classroom. I put my eyes on my paper, not looking up at what I was sure was a classroom of people staring at me.

After class Ms. Utz gave me back my phone, and I dashed out of the classroom. I had two BBMs from Jacob time-stamped after Ms. Utz took away my phone.

Jacob Schwartz:

U ok?

A few minutes later . . .

Jacob Schwartz:

Did something happen 2 ur phone?

As I left the history building, I barely watched where I was going as I typed him a message.

Sasha Silver:

Ugggh! Sorry!! Got caught by Utz and she took my phone. ☹ *But BBM me whenever u want. TTYL.*

I weaved through the students hurrying—like always—to sports or other after-school activities. It felt like a rush of relief when I stepped inside Orchard and closed the door behind me.

Quiet.

Finally.

I walked down the now fully-decorated fall hallway. Stephanie had decorated each hall table, put a wreath of real-looking leaves on her door, and had lit battery-powered candles at the end of the hall to make things feel cozy.

I opened my door and the room was empty. Brit would be back any second, though, since we both had to get ready for our riding lesson.

My phone buzzed and I pushed it on, expecting a BBM or text. Instead, it was an e-mail alert. All I had to do was read the subject of the e-mail before I tossed my phone on my bed and grabbed my laptop.

My finger pressed the on button hard, and I ran my hand over the mouse, back and forth, to try and wake the sleeping computer faster.

The subject of the e-mail kept running through my brain.

SASHA SILVER & ERIC RODRIGUEZ? A HOT NEW COUPLE AGAIN?

My computer finally came on and I went to the blog. The latest post, dated only minutes ago, had a photo of Eric and me standing in the hallway, smiling at each other. I could barely make myself read the text that was under the picture.

Look at who was spotted in the hall today! Small-town Sasha Silver with her former boy toy and total hottie Eric Rodriguez. But didn't they break up? Didn't mousy Sasha manage (ummm, how, seriously?) to snag *Jacob*? If they're as together as they've looked, I wonder how Jacob will feel that his GF is flirting with her old BF. Come on, Sasha. If you're going to do that, at least be smart and do it in private.

xx

"Are you *kidding* me?" I half screamed to no one.

This was beyond ridiculous. The gossip blogger had to be stopped. Or we were going to be expelled. I couldn't even start to think about that.

My door opened and Brit walked inside as I was rubbing my temples.

"Hey!" Brit said, grinning until she saw my face. Her smile disappeared. "What's wrong?"

"Oh, just a little something that the stupid gossip blogger just posted! Look." I shoved my laptop at Brit and picked up my phone. Even though I'd already talked to Jacob and hadn't done anything wrong, I still wanted to talk about it.

Brit read the post in seconds. "Oh, Sasha. I'm so

sorry! But you didn't do anything, and Jacob's *not* going to think you want to be back with Eric."

"I know he won't," I said. "But this is so wrong. And a photo? Really? Was that necessary?"

I needed gloss *stat*. I grabbed one from my special gloss bag that I only used for dates and going out. But this was an emergency. I applied a coat of peachy pink Dior gloss. That made me feel a little better.

Brit looked at the phone in my hand. "Go ahead and call Jacob. It'll make you feel better. We'll go to our lesson when you're done, okay? Just know that you're allowed to talk to whomever you want and the gossip blogger *is* going to be stopped."

I took a shaky breath. "Thanks, Brit. I won't be long on the phone—promise. We won't be late to our lesson."

Brit waved her hand. "Take your time. We can tack up two horses faster than anyone."

I smiled. "Now that's something that actually is true."

I hit Jacob's speed dial number, taking deep breaths while the phone rang.

"Hey," Jacob said. His voice was upbeat, and it sounded like he was walking somewhere—I could hear the wind.

"Hi," I said. "You might have already heard or read about it, but we got attacked by the gossip blogger today."

"What? What did it say?"

I paused. I knew Jacob would believe me, especially since I'd already told him about talking to Eric, but I was still a little scared.

"It said I was flirting with Eric in the hallway. There's a picture of us smiling at each other."

"Sasha, I'm so sorry. I know you didn't flirt with Eric—I wouldn't have said anything about if you hadn't brought it up. I trust you."

"I know you do. I just wanted to call you and make sure you knew that the post was up. I didn't want you to be surprised."

"That was sweet," Jacob said. "But I don't care what the gossip blogger said."

"I don't either. It hurt my feelings a little, though, that the blogger couldn't believe *I* was with you."

"What do you mean?" Jacob's tone dropped.

"It basically said that I was no one and how crazy it was that someone like me was dating you."

"Sasha, I can't even tell you how untrue that is. Whoever wrote that is obviously jealous of you. The blogger should have written the opposite—that I'm lucky to have someone like *you* interested in me."

"Jacob."

He couldn't have said anything else that could have made me feel that good.

"I mean it. When the gossip blogger is caught, I'll definitely have something to say."

"Defending my honor, huh?" I laughed.

Jacob joined me. "Most definitely."

I checked the time on the pool-colored wall clock. "I've got to go or I'll be late for my lesson. But I'll talk to you later."

"Have a good ride."

We hung up, and I raced to throw on the cleanest pair of breeches I could find. Brit had dressed while I was on the phone. She stood in front of our full-length mirror and pulled her hair into a low ponytail.

"Tell me again that the gossip blogger doesn't matter," I said to Brit.

She turned, finishing putting up her hair. "The gossip blogger does *not* matter. What does, is our lesson. Shake it off and focus." Brit's eyes met mine. "The blogger isn't going to help you at Huntington."

I pulled on my boots, knowing Brit was right. There

hadn't been a more important time to focus since I'd come to Canterwood. As Brit and I walked to the stable, I couldn't help but wonder—what if the blogger was a rider, too? What if it was a total bonus if the blogs distracted the targeted riders to cause them to be unprepared for Huntington?

8
CHARM'S FAVE

THE NEXT MORNING, IT WAS FOGGY AND gray for my riding lesson. I loved the sun, but this weather was fun too. I loved the moodiness of it and was thrilled that we were riding outside this morning. Charm would be especially happy once he realized what we were doing—cross-country.

"Hiya, gorgeous!" I said, peering into Charm's stall.

He looked up, his mouth full of hay.

I shook my head. "As if I'm surprised by that. But you do look very cute."

Charm chomped down on his hay and walked up to me, sticking his head over the stall door.

I put down his tack and grooming kit. I ran my hand down his blaze and kissed his soft muzzle.

"Missed you," I said.

Charm bumped his head into my shoulder and I laughed. "I think someone's ready to get out of his stall. C'mon."

Charm stepped back as I slid open the stall door and held onto his halter. It was one of my favorites on him. It was a soft brown leather that had his name engraved on a gold plate. My parents had gotten it for him for Christmas. Mom had even wrapped it in paper she'd found with carrots.

I put him in crossties and grabbed a hoof pick from my tack box. We had to be outside and ready in minutes. Charm was a perfect boy as I scraped his hooves, then started brushing him. In superspeed mode, I used his red rubber currycomb to get his growing winter coat under control. After that, a soft body brush made him shine and I combed his mane and tail until they were tangle free.

"Time for tack!" I said.

Ahead of me, I saw Brit pause with Apollo in the aisle. "Want me to wait?" she called.

"No way, but thanks," I said. "Go ahead. We'll be right there."

"Okay." Brit turned Apollo back toward the front of the stable and went outside.

I unclipped the crossties and slipped Charm's reins over his head and let them hang around his neck.

He took the bit without a second of hesitation, and I buckled the straps. I placed a dark green heavier saddle pad on his back and lifted my English saddle on top of it. Reaching under Charm's stomach, I grabbed the girth and tightened it. I put on my own helmet and cross-country protective vest.

Charm's big brown eyes got wider as he looked at my vest. He knew what it meant.

"That's right," I said, patting his neck after I pulled on my gloves. "We're going out on the trails!"

Charm started walking forward—without me!

"Whoaaa! Wait for me!" I grabbed his reins, laughing. "We're going, we're going."

I loved his excitement, though. It was adorable.

We got outside and the fog had lifted just enough so jumping in the woods and racing across the fields wouldn't be dangerous.

I stopped Charm beside Apollo and the two horses, both excited, sniffed muzzles. Heather, on Apollo's other side, was adjusting Aristocrat's martingale.

"Made it," I said, glad that I'd beat Mr. Conner. I did *not* want to be on stall mucking duty because I was late.

"Callie's not here yet, either, so don't worry," Brit said.

"That's no excuse," Heather said. "What possible reason could *you* have to be almost late?"

"Um, maybe because I had things to do," I said, shaking my head at her. "I wasn't late, so chill."

Heather glared at me for a second, then stared straight ahead as Callie and Black Jack walked out of the stable entrance and into the fog.

Callie mounted and the four of us waited in silence for Mr. Conner. After a few excruciatingly long minutes, Heather let out an enormous sigh and walked Aristocrat in front of us, pulling him around to face us.

"This is so pathetic," Heather said. Her eyes ran over each of us.

None of us said a word. I was too scared to and when I glanced over at Brit and Callie, it looked as though they were thinking the same.

"We're *the* YENT team," Heather said. "I don't care who hates who or if someone's mad because of a boyfriend or because someone borrowed her eyeliner and never gave it back. *Whatever.* We're about to compete at Huntington and if we're not even a team when we're at home, we're going to flop at our first show. Given."

I looked down at Charm's mane knowing she was right.

Heather held up a hand. "Please. Don't get me wrong. I'm *so* not saying we all have to be besties—I definitely don't want to go that far—but we have to act like a team because that's what we are. So we all"—Heather paused—"including myself, have to get over our issues and figure out how to make this work."

Brit, Callie, and I nodded simultaneously. Nothing needed to be said—everyone seemed to sense it. We had to do it.

Heather rejoined us in line and Aristocrat had just settled when Mr. Conner led Lexington, the gray gelding he was finishing training, out of the stable.

Mr. Conner got into the saddle, also wearing a protective vest and helmet, and rode up to us.

The second I saw his face, I knew something was wrong. He halted Lexington in front of us and stared us down. My heartbeat sped up and I tried not to panic. I hadn't done anything wrong, but he looked mad.

Not. Good.

"Before we start this morning's lesson," Mr. Conner said. "I want to address the blog post that went live yesterday. It directly targeted a member of our team in a hurtful way. I'd reiterate again that behavior such as the gossip blogger's is not tolerated at Canterwood Crest. The teachers and Headmistress Drake will be taking further action to uncover whoever is writing this blog. Callie, the headmistress is not sharing her suspicions with other students, so please keep this to yourself."

He looked at the four of us, and I'd never seen him so angry. Well, except for the time he'd caught me riding Charm at midnight in the stable.

"I want to say one final word on this matter," Mr. Conner continued. "If any of you know who is responsible for this, I hope you do the right thing and come forward. This negativity will slowly begin to disrupt activities such as sports, including ours, if it hasn't already."

Mr. Conner gave us one last hard gaze, then raised his chin. "Okay, let's get started. We're going to take a new cross-country path today. Instead of going through the woods behind the stable, we're going to head down the driveway and cross the road into a new field. We've gotten permission from the landowner, and Mike and I have checked the field several times. There are several great natural jumps and a change of scenery will be good for all of us."

Callie, Brit, Heather, and I smiled at each other—we couldn't help it. Anytime we got to ride in a new area, it was superexciting.

"If you're ready, let's go," Mr. Conner said.

"Ready!" the four of us chimed.

We circled our horses away from the stable, following Mr. Conner and Lexington down the driveway. The horses' metal shoes rang out on the concrete drive and their ears and eyes flicked from side to side, taking in the new view of campus. We'd only been outside of campus a few times on horseback, and I *loved* it.

The fog, still thick in some patches, was heavy enough that it covered the campus buildings that were in sight. Only the faintest glow of yellow lights from windows and streetlamps shone through.

We reached the end of the driveway, and Mr. Conner halted, raising his hand so we'd all stop.

"Please be extremely careful as we cross the road," Mr. Conner said. "The fog will make seeing any cars difficult."

"Yes, sir," we said.

"I'll go first," Mr. Conner said, looking over his shoulder at us. "When I get across, I'll direct you one at time to come to the other side. I don't expect there to be any cars, since this is a quiet street, but we're going to be extra careful."

Callie, Heather, Brit, and I waited at the end of the driveway while Mr. Conner peered down the winding road for cars. The trees that lined either side of the street were bare and crunchy leaves covered parts of the street.

Mr. Conner started Lexington forward and the gray moved at an easy walk. He was young and still green, but Mr. Conner was training him well. Mr. Conner walked him straight down the road toward the metal gate that would allow us access to the field. Lexington was yards from the gate when a loud *SQUAWK* and flapping of wings shattered the morning silence.

I jerked my head up and saw a *huge* black crow fly out of a tree just to Lexington's right. The gelding, already terrified from the noise, spooked. He let out a shrill neigh and rose into the air. I gasped, unable to move. Mr. Conner threw himself forward, trying to force his weight to push Lexington back onto the ground. But Lexington's body was vertical.

A horrible, scraping sound of horseshoes on concrete and leaves, wet from fog, rang in my ears.

Lexington, with red nostrils and white in his eyes, flipped onto his back—pinning Mr. Conner.

Callie, Heather, Brit, and I gasped.

"Mr. Conner!" Heather screamed.

There was a tangle of horse and rider. Mr. Conner managed to free himself from the saddle and was on his back on the road. As fast as Lexington had reared, he'd managed to roll onto his side and get his legs back under him. Shaky, he started to walk to the grass on the side of the road.

"Sasha, grab Lexington," Heather barked. "Brit, get off Apollo and go by Mr. Conner. Don't move him if he's hurt, but see if he can get off the road. Callie, go for help."

Callie turned Jack back toward the stable and let him race along the fence at a gallop.

Heather and I trotted our horses into the street. Heather rode a few yards down the one-way road, took off her cross-country vest, and put it on the road. It took me a second to realize what she was doing. The vest had reflective tape. If Mr. Conner couldn't move, any oncoming cars would see the tape and stop.

Brit kneeled by Mr. Conner. As I started for Lexington, I saw Mr. Conner sit up. My thudding heart slowed just a fraction. He couldn't be too hurt if he could sit up.

Lexington, shaken and scared, didn't try to bolt

when I eased Charm next to him and reached over to grab his reins.

"Easy, boy," I said. His sides were heaving and he had a scrape on his flank. I dismounted and stood between Charm and Lexington. I started to lead them toward Mr. Conner, Brit, and Heather, watching Lexington for any sign of injury. He seemed to be moving without any pain, and he wasn't favoring any of his legs.

"I'm okay, girls," I heard Mr. Conner say as I reached him. But his face was gray. I'd never seen him look like this. He was clutching his right leg. I choked back a sob when I looked at it. It was bent at an odd angle.

"You're not okay," Heather said. "Your leg—it's broken. You shouldn't even be sitting up—you always tell us that. But we *are* in the middle of the road. Can we help move you a few feet over onto the shoulder of the road?"

Mr. Conner, teeth gritted, nodded. "I want you girls out of the road. It's dangerous. The fog—"

He started to stand, trying to put his weight on his left leg and let out a low moan. Brit and Heather jumped to his side and put their arms around his sides, even though he towered over them. It took several agonizing steps, but Brit and Heather got Mr. Conner off the road and sitting in the grass while Apollo and Aristocrat stood beside them. Brit and Heather crouched next to Mr. Conner and I held Lexington and Charm.

"Callie went for help," I said. "Someone will be here any second."

"I'm sorry, girls," Mr. Conner said. "I tell you to be on alert every second and I should have been, too." His practiced eyes swept over Lexington. "How is he?" Mr. Conner asked me.

"I walked him and he moved fine," I said. "He's probably going to be sore, but he's not favoring anything."

That brought a hint of color back to Mr. Conner's face. "Thank you, all. You could not have been more mature and calm."

Hoofbeats thudded in the grass, increasing in sound. Through the lifting fog, Callie, Mike, and Doug rode over to us.

"An ambulance is on the way," Mike told Mr. Conner as he dismounted. "It will be here any second."

"Girls," Doug said. "You'll head back to the stable with me. I don't want the sirens to spook the horses. Mike's going to stay with Mr. Conner."

Mike handed Doug his horse's reins, and Doug looked at me. "Do you feel you can lead Lexington back? If you're nervous, I'll lead him."

I looked at Lexington, whose head was low. He felt bad for what he'd done—he wasn't going to act up again.

"I've got him," I said.

Doug nodded. "All right. Let's get back to the stable."

I felt awful leaving Mr. Conner. "Are you sure we can't stay?" I asked.

"No," Mr. Conner's voice was firm. "You all have been amazing. Go back to the stable with Doug. I'm fine with Mike."

We nodded, casting one look back at him before the four of us followed Doug at a walk across the road and down the driveway. No one said a word.

I'd never seen an injury like that happen, and it had definitely rattled me. Mr. Conner was so experienced, but he was leaving in an ambulance.

We got back to the stable and Doug turned to us. "Mr. Conner will be okay," he said, his tone reassuring. "I don't think any of you feel up to practicing this morning, so untack your horses and go back to your dorms to get ready for class."

"Will you text us the second you hear something about Mr. Conner?" Callie asked.

"Promise," Doug said. "You handled yourselves extremely well in an emergency—keep that in mind and try not to worry too much. The situation could have been much worse if you'd lost your cool."

He dismounted and led his horse and Mike's down the aisle. The four of us sat—frozen in our saddles.

"I've never seen Mr. Conner look like that," Callie whispered. "He was in so much pain. Oh, my God. I just keep seeing Lexington rearing, over and over in my mind."

Brit's face was pale. "I know. I don't even know if I *can* dismount. My whole body is shaking."

"He's going to be okay," Heather said, sounding as if she was trying to convince all of us. "We did everything right. Mike's there until the ambulance comes and all we can do now is wait to hear."

"But his leg . . . ," I started. It almost made me throw up to think about how it was bent. "It's definitely broken."

Heather couldn't dispute that. She just nodded. "I know." Her tone was soft.

"Maybe we can get out of our first class," Brit said. "I won't be able to concentrate anyway."

Heather hopped out of Aristocrat's saddle. "I think we should at least ask our teachers. Good idea."

"I'm going to untack Charm and just go to Mr.

Davidson's office," I said. "He's my first class this morning." I turned to Brit. "I'll BBM you if I don't have to go. And you let me know too, and we can meet up in our room."

"Sounds good," Brit said.

"You can come over to my suite if I'm able to get out," Heather said.

Brit and I nodded. I wanted to be surrounded by friends right now. The three of us dismounted, joining Heather on the ground.

I looked over, seeing sadness on Callie's face. She was going to Orchard too. To her single if she got out of class. She'd be alone.

"Callie?" I said.

"Yeah?" Her eyes were pink when she looked at me.

"If you get out of class and you, you know, want to, you should come wait for news with us at Heather's."

Callie blinked and chewed on her bottom lip. "That would be . . . great," she said, her voice soft. "Thank you." She looked at Heather. "Is that okay?"

"Definitely."

We all exchanged tiny smiles before we led our horses into the stable and toward their stalls. They didn't need to be groomed—just untacked.

Like a zombie, I untacked Charm and put away his gear. I came back to hug him extra tight. "I hope Mr. Conner's okay," I whispered. "He has to be."

As I walked back to Orchard, everything hit me. I cared about Mr. Conner more than I realized. He was an instructor I'd been seeing twice a day almost since I got to Canterwood. He pushed me to be a better rider and had made Charm and me a better team. I was as intimidated by him as I was inspired. The thought of him being away from the stable felt scary.

I wiped tears off my face, not even realizing I was crying until I got to the stairs of the English building.

I went inside and walked to Mr. Davidson's office. His door was closed, but the light was on inside.

I knocked, waiting for a response.

"Come in," he called.

"Hi, Mr. Davidson," I said, trying to stop sniffling.

"Sasha." Mr. Davidson got out of his chair and came around from behind his desk, putting a hand on my arm. "Sit down and let me get you a glass of water. You're pale."

His blue eyes stayed on me as he got me a plastic cup of water from the tank in his office.

He handed me the cup and sat at the edge of his desk

so he was in front of me. "What happened? Are you all right?"

I took a sip of the cool water, trying to calm my still racing heartbeat.

"Mr. Conner—he, he fell off his horse," I said, choking up as I said the words. "We were crossing the street and his horse reared and fell on him. My teammates and I got Mr. Conner and his horse off the road and got an ambulance."

Mr. Davidson covered his mouth. "Oh, my gosh. Sasha, that had to be terrifying. I'm so sorry. Is Mr. Conner all right?"

"I think he broke his leg,' I said, desperately trying not to picture it. "One of the grooms, Doug, is supposed to call us when he has news. It was"—I had to take a breath—"so scary. I've never seen anyone get hurt like that. Ever."

Mr. Davidson's eyes were sympathetic. "That's something no one should have to ever witness. Again, I'm so sorry. But it sounds as though you and your friends did all the right things. You might have saved his life."

I couldn't even think about that.

"I know I'm not sick, Mr. Davidson, but I wouldn't

be able to concentrate in class. Is there any way I can make up the—"

He smiled at me, shaking his head. "Sasha, I wouldn't ask you to come to class after that. You need to try and rest if you can, while you wait for news about your instructor. Please do not worry about class today. Okay?"

"Thank you. I really appreciate it."

Mr. Davidson nodded. "Of course, Sasha. I'll be on the alert for updates about Mr. Conner too. Are you all right getting back to your room?"

I finished the final sips of my water and tossed the cup in the tiny trash can beside me. "I'm fine."

"Let your dorm monitor know if you need anything, okay?" Mr. Davidson said.

"Okay. Thank you."

Mr. Davidson got up and opened the door for me.

I walked out of his office, starting to BBM Brit to tell her I was heading back to our room to change and then, hopefully, meeting her, Heather, and Callie at Heather's.

There was already a message on my phone.

Heather Fox:

No class 4 me. Come over whenever.

Sasha Silver:

Me either. Be there soon.

I swiped my hand across my eyes and pushed the button for the elevator. My legs weren't stable enough for stairs.

"Sasha?"

I looked up and saw Paige. Her green eyes, wide, searched my face.

"What happened?" she asked. "Are you okay?"

"No," was all I managed to choke out.

"Come here." Paige took my hand and slowly led me over to a bench at the end of the hallway, away from any student traffic that would soon fill the building.

Like nothing bad had ever happened between us, Paige put her arm around my shoulders and I leaned into her. The entire story came out and Paige rubbed my back, calming me down.

"Oh, Sasha," she said when I was finished. "I can't even imagine. I'm so, *so* sorry that happened to Mr. Conner and that you had to witness it. But I've been around Mr. Conner enough to know that he's going to be fine. You have to know that what you, Brit, Heather, and Callie did was something few students would have been able to do. *I* would have panicked. You didn't. You should be proud."

"Thank you," I said, looking at her for a second. "For saying that and for talking to me. You didn't have to."

"Sasha. I wanted to. I want us to be friends again. I—" Now it was Paige's turn to get teary. "I miss you. I miss being your friend. I miss movie nights. And TV marathons. And going to The Sweet Shoppe. Everything. I'm so sorry for what I did."

"I miss you," I said. "I miss all of that. You were my best friend and nothing's been the same since I moved out. You have to know that."

"Same thing for me," Paige said. "I love having Geena as my roommate, and you seem so happy with Brit—and I'm glad—but I miss us."

I leaned over, hugging Paige. "Me too."

After a few seconds, we pulled apart. "You've got to get to class," I said. "I don't want you to get in trouble."

"Only if you're okay," Paige said.

"I am now. Thanks to you."

"All I did was listen," Paige said. "I want to keep talking, if you do. Maybe a Sweet Shoppe date soon?"

"I'd love that."

We hugged again with promises to start BBMing to say hi until we set up our Sweet Shoppe meeting. Paige went back down the hall toward Mr. Davidson's classroom and I got in the elevator.

When I got closer to Orchard, my phone buzzed twice almost simultaneously.

Brit Chan:

My teacher was totally understanding. B in r room in 5.

Callie Harper:

I got excused from class. Changing then going 2 H's.

I wrote to Brit that I'd see her in a sec and to Callie that I was glad she got out of her first class and that Brit and I would meet her at the Trio's suite.

Twenty minutes later, the four of us were gathered in the Trio's living room.

"Did you tell Julia and Alison?" Callie asked. She was sitting cross-legged on the floor. We all had our phones on extra loud and in front of us so that there wasn't even a chance of us missing a call or text about Mr. Conner.

"I texted them," Heather said. "I didn't want them hearing misinformation and freaking out."

"Were they upset?" Brit asked. She and I were sitting on the couch.

Heather nodded. "They were. They both told me to BBM them the second we hear something. They're going to tell other riders as they see them in class."

"That's a good idea," I said. "It's hard to hear, but I'd

want to know from friends instead of hearing gossip and being shocked."

We were all quiet for several minutes. No one wanted to watch TV or read or do anything. None of us could concentrate.

"So this is what it took," Callie said. She shook her head. "I can't believe it took a serious accident for us to sit in a room and talk. I'm sorry."

"Me too," I said. "It never should have come to this. We're a team and we haven't been acting like it at all. I'm sorry, too."

Brit looked around at all of us. "I'm with Sasha. I made a lot of mistakes, and I'm not going to repeat them. I'm completely with this team."

From her spot on the recliner, Heather nodded. "I *might* have been a *little* immature about some stuff."

I looked at her. Heather had changed. The old Heather Fox would have ripped into us and not admitted to doing anything wrong. But it had actually been Heather who'd been the main force in pulling our team together and talking us into how important it was to be a team.

"All we can do now is be better in the future," I said. "There's no reason to beat ourselves up for what we've done."

Callie glanced at me. "Sasha's right. Mr. Conner's accident can't be for nothing. We have to take something away from it, and I think we got a message he'd be proud of."

We sat still, absorbing Callie's words.

"Hey," Brit said, her tone light. "Someone has a birthday tomorrow."

Heather sighed. "Don't remind me. I've been trying to forget about it. That means my mother will be invading campus tomorrow and throwing me a party I don't want."

Brit and I exchanged quick looks. Heather had no idea that we'd been working over BBM with Julia and Alison to still plan the movie-themed party she wanted. It was happening as a surprise after her mom's party.

"The night might be better than you think," I said, trying to cheer Heather up without giving away anything.

Heather's phone went off with a shrill ring. She almost fell out of her seat as she snatched it from the table.

"Hello?"

She listened nodding. "Okay. Uh-huh."

"Is it about Mr. Conner?" I whispered.

She shot me a look, then nodded her head *yes*.

"Thanks for calling. And we'll definitely ride cross-country with you this afternoon if that's what Mr. Conner wants. We're up for it."

She ended the call and looked at us. "He's going to be totally fine." The relief was audible in her voice.

"Omigod! Wheeew!" Callie said, leaning back and clasping her cheeks in her hands.

"He didn't suffer from any head or back trauma," Heather continued.

"You said he's *going* to be fine," I said. "What about his leg?"

The elation in the room went on insta-pause.

"It's broken," Heather said, taking a deep breath. "He'll be out of the hospital late tomorrow, and Mike said he'll be able to get around on crutches."

"That's awful," Brit said. "I feel so bad that he got hurt at all."

"Mr. Conner told Mike he still wants us to practice cross-country this afternoon, so we're not *all* spooked by this morning. He wants us to keep practicing for Huntington."

Huntington.

"This sounds *awful*," I said. "But if we're riding with Mike, will Mr. Conner be able to coach us?"

"Of course he will," Heather said. "From the ground. He won't be able to ride until after Thanksgiving break, possibly closer to Christmas."

It felt like I'd been punched in the stomach. Mr. Conner getting better was more important to me than any show. But this was our first season as YENT competitors and our instructor would be coaching us from crutches.

"Don't have a panic attack, Silver," Heather said. "It's *Mr. Conner*. He's going to coach us better with a broken leg than any of the healthy coaches."

"Heather's right," Callie said. "We've got Mike too. He's not a coach, but he'll be able to go on cross-country rides with us."

"This is going to make us all rely on each other for coaching when Mr. Conner can't be there," Brit said. "Going into Huntington, I don't know if that's necessarily a terrible thing."

No one disagreed.

9

BACK IN
THE SADDLE

AFTER WE GOT THE CALL ABOUT MR. CONNER, we split up the list of riders we had in our phones and told them the news about Mr. Conner. By the time we'd finished, it was time to get to our second class. I felt better throughout the afternoon about Mr. Conner's condition. But it felt weird not to have him on campus, even though I didn't see him during the day except for lessons: like I could still feel his absence.

I slogged through my classes and met Brit back in our room to change for our riding lesson.

"I'm nervous," I admitted. "I understand why Mr. Conner wants us to ride the same course with Mike so we're not afraid, but the accident just happened this morning."

Brit laced up brown paddock boots. "I feel the same way. I don't want to go anywhere near that spot. Especially not right now. But I trust Mr. Conner and I know he's right. We have to go or our fears will intensify."

Reluctantly, I got up off my bed and followed Brit out the door. At least the morning fog had lifted and the November sun was bright in the cloudless sky. Brit and I gathered our tack and separated to get Charm and Apollo ready, since the stable was packed. Everyone was talking about Mr. Conner's accident. Someone had put a giant piece of white poster board over his office door and there were scribbled notes for him to get better and come back. I made a mental note to sign it after my lesson.

"Sasha!" Nicole Allen, one of my riding friends, called after me. She brushed her blond curls from her heart-shaped face. "Thanks for texting me about Mr. Conner. Omigosh, I'm so glad that you and the rest of the YENT riders were there to help. Were you scared?"

"It was really scary," I said. "For a minute, I didn't think I'd be able to move, but all of us just snapped out of being afraid and knew we had to help him."

"That's amazing," Nicole said. "I put a poster board up on his door. Tell anyone you see to sign it."

I should have known it had been Nicole. She was so

sweet—she'd been the first person to welcome me to Canterwood when I'd arrived.

"It's a great idea—he'll love it," I said. "I'll definitely let people know."

"I've got to groom Wish, but talk to you later." Nicole smiled at me and headed off toward her gelding's stall.

As I walked toward Charm's stall, I made up my mind to keep him inside while I tacked him up. The stable was bustling with chatter about Mr. Conner, and I didn't want Charm getting nervous. Me either. Hearing about the accident over and over wasn't exactly something I wanted.

I put Charm's tack down on his wooden trunk and grabbed a body brush. It was all he'd need before our ride. He was clean enough from this morning.

"Hi," I said, my voice soft. He'd had a rough start to the day too, and I didn't want to startle him.

Charm looked up at me from the corner of his stall. His left hind leg was cocked in a relaxed position. Inside, I put my arms around his neck and breathed in his scent. It was my favorite—better than any body spray or perfume. Even Heather's expensive Burberry kind.

Charm smelled like fresh, clean hay and sweet grain. I kissed his cheek, something he sometimes wouldn't let me do in front of his friends, and rubbed his blaze.

"We're going to go for a cross-country ride with everyone and Mike," I said. "Mr. Conner broke his leg this morning."

Charm looked at me, seeming to listen.

"I'm kind of scared to go back to there." I rubbed my eyes, trying to block out the images of what had happened this morning. "It's what Mr. Conner wants, though, so we have to do it."

Charm, always in tune with my feelings, rubbed his head against my arm like a giant dog.

"Sweet guy," I said. "Thank you. Let's get you tacked up and get out there."

It only took minutes to get him ready and soon, we were heading down the aisle to meet Mike and his mount outside the stable.

We passed Trix's stall, and Julia had the mare tied outside. "Heard you're the big hero who rescued Mr. Conner," she said, unsmiling.

"No," I said, shaking my head. "I grabbed Lexington. Didn't Heather tell you what all of us did?"

Julia rolled her eyes and whisked a dandy brush over

Trix's bay coat. "Yeah. Whatever. She said the YENT riders got Mr. Conner help."

Sometimes, I didn't understand this girl. She went from hot to cold with me in seconds for no reason I could figure out.

"Look. Are you . . . *mad* about something?" I asked.

Julia yanked the knot out of the lead line on the iron bar on Trix's stall and started to lead the mare away from me.

"Nope," she called over her shoulder. "Everything's *perfect*. I have zero reason to be upset."

I sighed. I didn't have time to go after her, not that I really wanted to, or figure out what was going on. If she had some sort of complex that we'd "saved" Mr. Conner then that was her problem. Julia usually wasn't a huge attention hog, but maybe she wished she'd been in on this. I didn't understand why, since what I'd seen had been horrible.

Enough, I told myself. *You don't have time for this.*

Charm and I resumed walking down the busy aisle. Outside, Brit, Callie, Heather, and Mike were all mounted. I got into Charm's saddle and instinctively tightened the straps on my cross-country vest.

"We're going to have a good, but fun workout,"

Mike said to us. He was riding Willow, a sweet strawberry roan school horse. "I imagine you're all feeling a little nervous and that's normal. But we're going to take things slow. Going back to the place of the accident and doing the cross-country you'd had planned for this morning is the best way to get rid of your fears. Okay?"

We all nodded, silent.

"I understand that this morning was extremely traumatic. If none of you feel you're ready to go back, I understand. Doug's in the outdoor arena, and he'll be more than happy to add you to any class he's teaching. You don't have to do this."

But we did. At least, *I* did.

"I can handle it," I said.

Everyone else chimed in with a similar response.

"Okay, then. Follow me down the drive, and we're going to cross the road together," Mike said. He squeezed his legs against Willow's side and the two started away from the stable and down the school's driveway.

Together, Heather, Brit, Callie, and I moved our horses forward. We reached the end of the driveway in what felt like seconds. There was a collective hesitation among us as we reached the end of the drive.

"It's okay, girls," Mike said, looking back at us. "Let's get the hard part over."

For the first time, moving as a team, we followed Mike and crossed the road together. We reached the grass and waited for Mike to open the gate. With ease, he leaned down from Willow's back and unlatched the metal gate. He walked her forward, swinging open the gate for us. We rode through and waited for Mike to latch the gate.

He stopped Willow in front of us, his freckled face already tinted red from the cold November breeze. I was glad I'd put on my wool coat and had put on Charm's warmest saddle pad. I dug into the zipper pocket in my coat and pulled out Tropical Punch Lip Smacker gloss. So I was kind of a nervous glosser . . .

"We're going to start with a trot across the field, then we'll canter for a couple of miles up and down a few hills to keep building stamina," Mike said. "We'll encounter a few low fences and hedges along the way, then we'll reach the woods. Once we get there, I'll explain what you'll come to next."

Mike smiled at us and adjusted his chin strap. "Ready?"

"Ready!"

And I was. The fear I'd felt about riding had disappeared once we'd reached the other side of the road. We had to be ready for Huntington—and cross-country was my favorite thing to do with Charm. This was going to be fun!

Mike let Willow into a trot and the four of us spread out our horses—there was plenty of room in the open field. I loved how the grass, crunchy from the cold air, sounded beneath Charm's hooves. It looked as if the field stretched for miles and only an occasional tree dotted the grounds.

Charm kept a smooth trot and with every minute that passed, I relaxed and enjoyed the ride more. I looked over at Brit to my right and Heather on my left. Both of them had calm looks on their faces—I couldn't see Callie but I had no doubt that she was the coolest of all of us.

"Let's canter," Mike called.

Yes!

I stopped posting and sat deep in the saddle, preparing to canter. Charm knew what was coming. I gave him an inch of extra rein and slid my hands a little higher up along his neck. He was cantering in two strides. I swayed gently in the saddle, moving with him.

Brit, glancing over, grinned as Apollo drew even with

us and all of our horses kept pace with one another.

The flat field started to ascend into a gentle incline. I leaned slightly over Charm's neck and tapped my heels against his sides. I didn't want him to slow—he had to keep the same speed going uphill. And the zillions of hours we'd spent practicing at Briar Creek and Canterwood paid off. Charm had no trouble maintaining a steady, even rhythm up the hill. His breathing didn't get heavier as the hill got steeper with every minute that passed.

After a few minutes, the ground leveled and the wind roared in my ears as Charm cantered. He tossed his head and snorted, invigorated by the practice.

Strides ahead, I watched Mike and Willow approach a row of brush. Willow lifted into the air, clearing the brush. Right behind Mike, Heather and Aristocrat, then Callie, then Brit cleared the hedge.

Now *this* was the awesome part. At the right second, I lifted into the two-point position and Charm rose into the air. He took the brush as if he was stepping over a crack in the driveway, and I could feel the eagerness in his body to jump more.

We cleared four more hedges, and Mike led us over a fallen tree that had its branches sawed off to prevent any injury to the horses' legs.

Woods were now visible in the distance, and we followed Mike's lead as he slowed Willow to a trot, then a walk a few paces later.

"Everyone doing okay?" Mike asked.

"Totally," Heather said. The rest of us nodded.

"Great," Mike said, patting Willow's shoulder. "We're about to enter the woods. They're perfect for cross-country. You won't encounter anything out of the ordinary, so don't worry. There will be a few logs, a creek that's narrow enough to jump, a bank, and lots of twists in the trail. Stay on alert for any deer because Mr. Conner and I saw a few last time we were here."

We nodded at him. At first, it had felt weird to take instruction from Mike, but he was a natural instructor. I liked riding with him.

"Stay single file with plenty of space between your horses," Mike said.

Behind him, we got into line. I fell behind Mike, Heather was after me, then Brit, and finally Callie.

We started at a posting trot into the woods. All of the trees were bare, so the horses didn't have to adjust to a low light. Charm, with both ears pointed forward, trotted along the dirt path. He loved this. We made several bends and ducked under a low-hanging tree branch as we followed Mike.

Mike and Willow leaped over a foot-high log, and we all did the same without a problem. Skinny branches on the bare trees surrounding both sides of the trail wavered in the wind. A few birds chirped, but the only sound I focused on was Charm's hoofbeats.

"Slow canter," Mike called back to us.

I let the leather reins slide through my fingers and Charm moved into a canter, not rushing or trying to get more rein.

We jumped two more logs and started down a slight hill. We slowed the horses to a trot, and I leaned back in the saddle. Charm took careful steps through the dirt until the ground leveled again. Mike and Willow started cantering, and I let Charm follow their pace. A few strides ahead, I saw the creek Mike had mentioned.

Mike pointed Willow at the narrowest part and the mare gathered herself and cleared it without hesitation.

Charm, excited about jumping and probably wanting to show off in front of his friends, approached the jump with an extra bounce in his stride. I did a half halt, not wanting him to get too excited and out of control, and he listened.

I counted down the strides, not wanting to end up in the freezing water.

Four, three, two, one, now!

I leaned forward in the saddle and Charm lifted into the air, his body suspended over the creek for a brief but amazing second. He landed easily on the other side, his hooves sinking a little bit into the soft dirt.

I heard Heather and Aristocrat land behind us, and Charm and I kept cantering. We swept around a sharp corner on the path and jumped a line of brush.

Charm was doing great! He'd made any anxiety I'd had disappear, and every stride we took reminded me how much I loved riding and being with Charm—not just cross-country. I was happy with Charm no matter what we were doing.

After a few more bends in the trail, we exited the woods. Mike slowed Willow to a trot. The mare, winded, shook out her mane and pranced for a few strides as he slowed her.

"We'll trot back across the field for half of the ride back and walk the final leg to the stable," Mike said. "How do you and your horses feel?"

"I'm great and so is Aristocrat," Heather said.

"Same here," Brit said. She gave Apollo rein to stretch his neck. The gray gelding's coat had darkened from sweat—just like the rest of the horses—but none of them looked too tired.

I ran a hand along Charm's neck, paying attention to his gait. I hadn't felt him take a single misstep, but I wanted to make sure he was okay. Each of Charm's hooves felt as if it touched the ground with the same force, and I didn't feel him favoring any of his legs. I'd walk him out for any possible soreness tomorrow morning. Charm was in great shape, though, and I didn't expect him to have any problems.

The five of us went back to the stable, discussing our rides with Mike. Mr. Conner had trained him well, and I just knew that one day, Mike would be teaching advanced and YENT classes.

I made sure Charm was cool and shiny before I left him in his stall. There was one thing left to do before I went back to Orchard. I took a turn down the side hallway and stopped in front of Mr. Conner's dark office. The poster board Nicole had put up was almost full with notes and signatures of all different colors of pens and markers. Nicole, smart girl, had put a can of a dozen pens and markers for everyone to use.

I looked through them and picked up a navy blue glitter pen. There was a tiny open space near the bottom left corner. I uncapped the pen and turning sideways a bit, I didn't need a moment to think about the message I wanted to write.

Mr. Conner—I'm sorry you got hurt, but know that if nothing else, it made a group of riders into a team. ~Sasha

10
LEGENDARY FOR . . . CANTERWOOD?

WHEN BRIT AND I GOT BACK TO OUR ROOM, we showered and sat together on the floor, a sparkly metallic folder spread open in front of us.

"Julia and Alison should be here in a few minutes," Brit said. "Then we'll have everything set for Heather's real party."

"I'm so glad we're doing it for her," I said. "She's acting like she's not upset or nervous about her mom coming, but she is. Wait until you meet Mrs. Fox. You won't believe how awful she really is."

Brit frowned. "That's rough. And you said her dad's horrible, too, isn't he?"

"Unfortunately. He's a total stage parent. All he wants Heather to do is practice. It's the only thing he wants her to excel at. But, also like Mr. Fox, he's not coming to her party."

"*What?*" Brit's mouth opened a little. "He's not coming to his daughter's thirteenth birthday party? Not even to see her?"

"Nope. Heather told me. She's glad he's not coming, but she's still hurt at the same time."

"Well, we're going to give her an amazing movie party. It'll make her forget all about her parents."

Someone knocked on our door and I stood up, opening the door for Julia and Alison.

"Hey," they both said. They were both dressed in cropped pajama pants, Havaianas, and VS Pink hoodies.

"C'mon in," Brit said, waving them over.

We all sat down next to Brit.

"How did you sneak away from Heather?" I asked. "She always knows *everything*."

Alison laughed. "True. Originally, we were going to tell her we were going to study at the library, hoping she wouldn't want to go. But we got sooo lucky because Troy called and they'll be on the phone for, like, ever."

That made everyone grin.

"Perfect," I said. "Let's run though final details and we're set."

Brit and I had been keeping all of the party info at our room since we didn't want to risk Heather finding it in the Trio's suite.

I pulled out the checklist.

"Here's what we've got," Brit said, looking over at the list. "Alison picked up the movies, and they're in our closet. Julia's already got the popcorn, movie candy, and big plastic cups for soda."

Both girls nodded.

"Sasha took a piece of poster board and made it into an ADMIT ONE movie ticket for Heather that we'll give her as a card. We talked to Stephanie and got the okay to sleep over in your suite for a night and to stay up late, even though it's a school night."

"I also got the delivery of streamers and a happy birthday sign from my Internet order," I said. "Plus, birthday candles and everything else we need to throw a real party."

"Yay!" Alison said, bouncing on the floor. "She's going to looove this. I'm so excited!" She turned to Julia. "Aren't you, Jules?"

Julia smiled, but it was thin. "Yeah, I'm excited. But I'm *really* into her mom's party, honestly. I know how Heather feels about her, but her mom throws killer parties. This one is going to be epic. Legendary for Canterwood and we're going. I ordered my dress from Saks the second Heather told me her mom was throwing it."

"Saks?" I asked. My gaze darted from Brit to Alison. I'd planned on wearing a cocktail dress I'd gotten from Macy's before school had started.

"Where else would I get a dress?" Julia asked with a snort. She shot me a glare. "Please tell me you did *not* get a dress from, like, Target or something."

"Excuse you," I said. "I like Target, first of all, so get over it. But no, I have a dress from Macy's."

"I got mine from there, too," Alison chimed in, shooting me an *ignore Julia she's being mean* look.

"And mine's from a vintage store when I went to New York City last summer," Brit said. "I think our dresses are going to get us in the door." She directed the last comment at Julia.

Julia stared at Brit for a second, then grabbed the list. "Did we cover everything? I've got a zillion things to do, and it seems like we're ready."

"We just got here," Alison said. "Don't you want to take, like, two more minutes to at least make sure our best friend's party is perfect?"

"Chill, Alison," Julia said. "Everything's covered. We're just going over the same stuff now."

"Don't tell me to chill," Alison snapped.

Ummm, whoa. I'd never seen Alison talk like that to Julia. She always deferred to her. Maybe she'd finally had enough of Julia's recent mood swings.

"This is Heather's party. I'm staying until everything's set," Alison continued. Her brown eyes never looked away from Julia's face, which, by the way, was getting redder by the second. "Go if you want. I'll see you back in our room."

Julia hesitated. Her gaze flitted from Brit and me to Alison. "Fine," Julia said, "See you back in our room."

She grabbed her purse and stomped out of the room. When the door was closed, Brit and I looked at Alison.

"Believe me, I wish I knew what was going on," Alison said. "Julia's been in a bad mood for a while. I'm guessing it's probably because she didn't make the YENT. But she knows she can try out again and what a good rider she is."

"It's weird," I said. "She was starting to become my friend and now she's back to hating me most of the time. I've never seen her talk to you like that, either."

Alison snuggled into her hoodie. "I'm sure she'll come out of it. She might be having problems with Ben or her parents or even class stuff that she's not talking to us about."

"Total possibility," Brit said. "There's nothing more we can do. She'll either start being nice again or she won't."

The three of us went back to looking over the details of Heather's surprise party. Alison left about half an hour later, when we were all satisfied that things were in good shape and ready to go for tomorrow.

After Alison left, I opened my closet door and pulled out the dress I wanted to wear. The black cocktail dress was simple, but the pretty lace straps gave it something special. With the right jewelry, it felt appropriate for Heather's party.

"This is okay, isn't it?" I asked Brit.

"It's more than okay," Brit said. "It's beautiful!"

I held up the dress in front of me and looked in the mirror. "This has to be okay—the party's tomorrow. I think with kitten heels and the right jewelry, it'll be perfect."

Brit walked toward her desk, getting ready to start on homework. "Don't let Julia get inside your head. She's ridiculous. You have no reason to listen to anything she says."

"Thanks, Brit. *I* love my dress, so who cares it's not from Barneys?"

That made Brit smile. "Exactly." She sat on her desk chair, taking textbook out of her book bag and putting them onto her desk. "I've so much homework tonight. Don't teachers know that we're supposed to sleep, too?"

"And you're not the only one, trust me. We'll both be doing homework all night."

I picked up my own bag and started getting my own homework ready. There was something in almost every subject. Ugh. I'd started for my desk chair, when my phone buzzed.

I opened BBM and there was a message from Jacob.

Jacob Schwartz:

I heard abt Mr. Conner. R u ok?

Homework could wait a few minutes. Just a few.

Sasha Silver:

I'm ok bc he's not srsly hurt. He DID break his leg, which is bad, but @ least he'll be back tomorrow.

Jacob Schwartz:

I heard you were pretty awesome.

Sasha Silver:

Aw, thanks. ☺ But rlly, it was my entire team. And srry I didn't BBM u abt it. Lots of things have been happening today.

Jacob Schwartz:

Don't worry abt it! I know ur busy. H's party is 2mrw, right?

Sasha Silver:

Yup. U sure you don't mind being my plus 1?

I'd asked Jacob over BBM a few days ago if he wanted to go with me. His feelings about Heather were mixed. He hated all the mean things she'd done to me, but he knew we were kind of friends now.

Jacob Schwartz:

R u kidding? I better go—my mom bought and shipped a tux. JK. ☺ I mean, I know I have to wear the tux, but it's worth it 2 b w/u.

Sasha Silver:

<3 Thanks. I'm rlly glad ur going. It'll b fun—we always find a way 2 have a good time 2gether.

Jacob Schwartz:

Def. I'm gonna get started on hmwk, but I'll c u 2mrw nite.

We said good-bye, and I plugged in my phone to charge. I needed a charger of my own—called caffeine— to get me through all of this homework.

Who knows how many hours later, Brit and I closed our books at the same time.

"Done," I said, stretching my arms above my head.

"Sooo done," Brit said. "I would have finished it in the morning if I hadn't been able to pull it off tonight. There was so much!"

I went to my dresser and pulled out cozy purple pajama pants and an oversized T-shirt. "I'm changing and going to bed. I'm exhausted."

"Me too."

My phone buzzed just as I started into the bathroom. I ignored it, deciding to check it when I came out. I washed my face, brushed my teeth and hair and got into my cozy clothes.

When I came out, Brit was on her laptop.

"I thought you were done," I said.

"I am. I just got a text alert that the gossip blog was updated."

"Oh, great."

I hurried to stand behind Brit, and I read over her shoulder.

HAPPY BIRTHDAY TO THE QUEEN!

So tomorrow's the invite-only überexclusive birthday bash for the Queen of Eighth Grade. Didn't get an invite? Only you and most of your friends didn't get one. Don't blame the Queen, however. Her mother, who has planned every aspect of the party, will descend upon Canterwood Crest tomorrow to make sure everything is perfect for her Park Avenue Princess. This swanky soirée is so hard to get into, even her best friends were probably up for consideration for invites. But don't worry—you'll see pictures of the gorgeous dresses, hot guys, stunning ballroom and a few other party-worthy shots later on this blog. Check back soon.

xx

I didn't even want to read it again—it made me sick and think of the looming consequence of expulsion.

"Heather's going to *freak*," I said.

Brit shut her laptop, turning around in her chair to face me. "No kidding. When she finds out who's blogging—and she will unless someone else does first—she's going to kill them."

"I don't even want to talk about it anymore," I said, pulling back my covers and throwing myself into bed. "It's ridiculous and I'm over it. It's disgusting and Headmistress Drake has to do something soon. She just has to."

"She will," Brit said as she headed into the bathroom. "The blogger will be caught."

11

EPIC PARTY . . . ?

ON WEDNESDAY, I SAW HEATHER A FEW times in the hallway. Every time, she had one of two expressions—fury or defeat. I almost told her about the real party we were planning just to cheer her up and get her through her mother's party. But I knew Brit, Alison, and Julia would kill me if I told her, so I didn't say a word.

After class, I went to my riding lesson and saw Mr. Conner for the first time since the accident. He was on crutches and he sat in a director's chair for our lesson, but he still barked instructions and didn't let up on us. I was glad. I'd been worried that he'd be in pain and not up for teaching. But he was the same Mr. Conner—just with crutches. He might have made us work even harder than usual.

I hurried across campus after cooling, feeding, and untacking Charm. I passed the ballroom, and there were giant black vans parked in front and people were carrying tables and boxes out of the vans and into the ballroom.

Heather's party started in a couple of hours, and I could only imagine the pressure Mrs. Fox was putting on all the people she'd hired to finish on time and make everything perfect.

Brit was already in our room when I got there.

"Time to start getting ready?" I asked, as I pulled off my coat and boots.

She closed her phone, nodding. "This is *not* the party to make a late entrance."

I studied her face—noting her flushed cheeks. "Are you going with Andy?"

Brit had been going back and forth about her answer. She said he'd asked her a couple of days ago, but she was still thinking about it. She was being extra cautious and thinking things through, trying to decide if now was the time to start seriously dating with all that we had going on. I didn't want to tell her what to do, but I thought that she should go out with him. Andy was a rider, so he understood her commitment to the YENT and wouldn't make Brit feel as if she was neglecting him to practice.

Brit smiled. "I said yes. He's really excited—it's so cute. He got a tux and everything."

"Yay! I'm *so* glad you decided to go with Andy. You guys will have an amazing time. I know it."

"I think we will." Brit glanced at our bedside clock. "If we get there on time."

"How about I shower first, superfast, then you, and while you're showering I'll dry and start to flatiron my hair. We can get dressed and do makeup together."

"Perf. And accessories."

"Definitely."

I grabbed my robe off my closet hook. "Be right out."

Inside the bathroom, I turned the water on steaming hot. I hadn't been to a party with Jacob in a long time and certainly never anything this fancy or as an official couple. I wanted to look perfect. I opened the bathroom cabinet and pulled out the expensive, special occasion shampoo Brit and I used only once in a while. I put the bottles of Bumble and bumble Gentle shampoo and Super Rich conditioner on the shower ledge. I also felt a body scrub was definitely necessary—Bliss, in Blood Orange + White Pepper. It always made my skin supersoft and smell pretty.

I undressed and hopped into the shower. I didn't take too long, so Brit would have plenty of time and lots of hot water. Brit showered after me, and we both started getting dressed.

"We definitely need to put on our dresses at the last minute," Brit said. "Otherwise, I'm sure I'll get makeup or something on mine."

"Me too."

We climbed onto our beds and started doing our makeup. I applied tinted moisturizer first, then my fave CoverGirl foundation. I did my eyes next— lining them with my sharpened-down-to-a-nub MAC kohl pencil; the thin black line above and under my eyes made them pop. I wanted my makeup to be soft, so I used my dual eye shadow—Like Mink—from Clinique. It was dark brown on one side and shim- mery, like sand, on the other. I dusted the lighter color almost up to my eyebrows and used my eye shadow brush to put a dusting of the darker color over my lids.

"Can I use your eyelash curler?" Brit asked. "Mine's being weird."

I tossed her the curler and she made her lashes flip upward.

I coated mine with black mascara, then dusted my cheeks with my fave Nars blush. A few dots of concealer made red spots on my chin vanish and a dusting of powder over my T-zone took away any shine. I applied a coat of my special going-out gloss from Tarina Tarantino's candy cameo line (thanks for the Sephora gift card, Mom!) and checked my makeup in the mirror. I looked as ready as I could be.

"You look so great!" Brit said. She gave me a once-over. "Wow. Your eyes look especially gorgeous."

"Thanks," I said, looking at her just-finished makeup. "You too. I love how you did your blush. You have super-model cheekbones."

Brit shook her head. "So not true, but thank you anyway."

We went through our box of shared accessories picked out earrings for both of us and a necklace for Brit.

"Your charm bracelet is perfect, and it goes so well with the skinny silver hoops."

"And I love your heart pendant," I said. "It hangs in just the right spot with your v-neck dress."

"We're going to be the hottest people at the party," Brit said. She giggled. "Heather might kick us out."

I laughed. "Total possibility."

We blow dried and flatironed our hair until it was straight and smooth. After a coat of shine spray, it was time to grab shoes and go. Jacob and Andy were meeting us there.

12

HAPPY BIRTHDAY, HEATHER!

BRIT AND I ARRIVED AT THE BALLROOM, invites in hand, and handed them to the doorman slash bouncer-looking guy at the door. I thought Heather had been joking when she'd said we'd need the invites to get in. But she'd been serious. We'd never have gotten a heeled foot in the door if we'd been without the invitations.

We handed the pieces of paper to a tall guy in a black suit and tie with an outstretched hand. He scanned our invites, almost as if he was checking to make sure they weren't fake, and then waved us inside.

A coat checker took our coats, and Brit and I took a simultaneous deep breaths—looking at each other. I couldn't stop feeling a little nervous—I'd never been to a party like this.

Ever.

We walked down the gleaming hallway, which had just been polished, and Brit opened the door to the ballroom. It seemed as if everyone else had the same theory we'd had about not wanting to be late. The ballroom was full. People from our class, and a few other students from ninth grade, were standing by a buffet table with a dozen platters of food.

"Is that *lobster*?" I whispered to Brit, not wanting to sound dumb.

"I think so. Wow."

Everything was decorated in deep purple and silver. Mrs. Fox had known exactly what she was doing—picking out a color like purple that stood for royalty. There were deep, cushy purple chairs and couches placed around the walls and corners of the ballroom. Silver, sparkly spirals dangled from the ceiling. The black and white marble floor was slick under my heels, and it caught reflections from the lights. Waitresses carrying trays of sparkling cider in champagne flutes moved through the room, offering drinks to the students. The fifty or so students were all dressed according to the invitation. The girls were in gorgeous dresses and there wasn't a guy without a tux. Shoes shined, diamonds sparkled, and it looked like a party where I didn't belong.

But it's Heather's, I told myself. There wasn't any reason to be nervous.

In the back of the room, on the biggest table was a gift pile for Heather. Brit and I hadn't brought our presents for Heather—we were taking the risk of her publicly decapitating us to make tonight's secret party even better.

Seated in one of the purple chairs with Troy and Alison sitting on either side of her, I spotted the birthday girl.

"Let's go say hi and then look for our guys," I said to Brit.

"Good plan."

We weaved through the students who were talking or dancing to music.

"Happy birthday!" Brit and I said when we reached Heather.

She looked stunning. She wore a short, fire-engine red spaghetti strap dress with black tights and heels. Diamond studs glittered from her ears and she wore a silver necklace that knotted around her throat. Her blond hair was curled into soft waves that brushed against her shoulders.

"Thanks," Heather said. "Mom outdid herself, huh?"

I nodded. "Um, yeah. It's insane in here. Where . . ."—I decided to lower my voice—"is she?"

Heather laughed and took Troy's hand. "Are you kidding? Please, Silver. I thought you'd know better. She split the second she saw everything was in perfect order."

Troy squeezed Heather's hand, an uncomfortable look on his face. "Want me to grab you a drink?" he asked her.

"Please," Heather said, smiling at him.

"I'll go with you," Alison said.

He smiled at all of us before heading for the drinks. He hadn't been with Heather for too long, so the talk about her mom probably made him uncomfortable.

"Did she hang out with you before the party started?" Brit asked.

I already knew the answer, though.

Heather's blue eyes were pale, pool blue. "She came to throw a Fox-worthy party. Then she left. Whatever. It's not like we're BFFs or anything. I'm glad she left."

Heather didn't fool me at all. Mrs. Fox had hurt her feelings. Again. Part of what Heather had said *was* true— they didn't get along and it would have been awkward between them. But it was a big birthday for Heather and her mother hadn't cared enough to stay. I doubted

Mr. Fox had even called or texted Heather two words about today. It made me sad and angry at the same time.

"Well, guess what?" I said. "If she's not here that means you can leave whenever you want. No one's here to make you stay."

That made Heather perk up a little. "True. Very true." She looked toward the drink table where Troy and Alison were almost at the front of the line.

"I want to stay for a little while because it's cool to be at a party with Troy," Heather said. "And he's having fun."

"Do whatever *you* want," Brit said. "It's your birthday. We're going to let you hang with Troy and go find Jacob and Andy."

"Oooh," Heather said. "So Andy *is* here for you. I knew it!"

Brit's eyes looked around the room. "You've seen him? He's here?"

Heather and I giggled at Brit's questions.

"He told me happy birthday a few minutes ago," Heather said. "I think he's probably chilling with Jacob, Ben, and some of the other guys."

I smoothed my dress when she said Jacob's name. He hadn't seen me in this dress before. I hoped he liked it.

Brit did the same—smoothing her vintage black dress with a keyhole back.

"Speaking of Ben," I said, sitting on the arm of Heather's chair. "Where's Julia? I haven't seen her."

Heather shrugged, sighing. "I have no clue. She didn't leave with Alison and me. She claimed she wasn't ready yet, even though she clearly was. She kept changing her mind about shoes."

"We've all been there," Brit said. "I'm sure she'll be here any second."

Troy and Alison, with champagne flutes and snacks in hand, returned.

Troy handed a glass to Heather, giving her a kiss on the cheek. Heather's face turned the same shade as her dress and she managed to utter a thank you.

"Have fun and we'll see you guys later," I said.

Alison, Troy, and Heather said bye to us. Brit and I started at the front of the room, looking for Jacob and Andy.

"We might have to BBM them," I said, only half joking.

"Total possibility," Brit said.

We reached a semi-empty space of the ballroom, where we could finally see, and Jacob and Andy were with Ben and a few other guys, just as Heather had predicted. I couldn't wait to get close to him. But my feet felt rooted to the floor. All I could do was stare at him.

I'd never seen him so dressed up. His black tux made him look beyond gorgeous. He had a crisp white button-down shirt on underneath and a dark green tie that made his eyes look even greener. He'd combed his hair, but still left it loose in that California surfer and Jacob—like way.

"Jacob looks so hot," I said to Brit. "Whoa."

"He looks great," Brit said. "And so does Andy."

Reluctantly, I shifted my gaze to Andy. Like Jacob, he was in a black tux and white shirt. He'd chosen a red tie that popped.

"Andy looks great, Brit. C'mon."

Brit was a half step behind me as we made our way over to the guys. Jacob was the first to see us. Immediately, he walked away from the guys and reached for my hand.

"Sasha," he said. "You look beautiful."

I always believed it when he said it.

"Thank you. I love your tux."

Jacob ran his hand over the sleeves, grinning as he pretended to brush dust off them. "This old thing?"

We smiled, looking at each other. I knew teachers were milling around as chaperones, but I didn't care. Jacob put his hands on my hips and touched his lips to mine. The kiss only lasted seconds, but it sent tingles through my body that lasted long after we weren't touching.

"I'm glad you're here," I said. "Doesn't this place look amazing?"

Jacob nodded. "It's Mrs. Fox's handiwork, that's for sure. I've never seen the ballroom look like this."

"Want to get drinks?" I asked.

"Definitely."

Before we walked away, I looked over at Brit. She and Andy had their heads bent together, already deep in conversation. She'd be totally fine if I left her alone.

Jacob and I took each other's hands and before we reached the drink line, a waitress offered us a tray of sparkling cider.

We each took a flute and sipped the drink.

"This is definitely *not* a Coke and pizza party," Jacob said. "Did you check out the food yet?"

"I saw it when I walked in," I said. "Fan-cy."

"Kind of in a scary way?" Jacob asked.

"Very," I giggled, looking at the mounds of translucent orange and black balls of caviar.

We finished our cider and put the glasses with the rest of the empty ones.

Jacob turned to me, a smile on his face. "We're doing everything we're supposed to at a party like this," Jacob said. "We've had a drink, complained that there's food that we probably can't pronounce . . . but there's one thing we haven't done yet."

I tilted my head to look at him. "And what might that be?"

Jacob took my hand, pulling me to an empty spot on the floor. "Dance," he said.

There was nothing I wanted to do more.

We danced to a pop song that I knew every word to, laughing and talking the entire time. The music changed to a slow song and, without even thinking about it, Jacob and I moved closer to each other. I put my head on his shoulder, his body warm against mine.

"This is perfect," I said, my voice soft. The second I said it, I hoped he wouldn't think I was being cheesy.

"It's more than perfect," Jacob said. His tone was gentle. "Everything always feels like that when I'm with you."

I had no words to respond. I wished I was smarter— that I had the right thing to say. Something as meaningful as what he'd just said.

"I don't know what to say," I said, deciding to be

honest. "Except that I feel that way too, and I wouldn't want to be anywhere else right now."

Jacob pulled me closer to him, and I smiled into his shoulder when another slow song started to play.

This may have been a party that Heather never wanted, but I couldn't help it—I was glad to be here. With Jacob.

13

SPEECHLESS

AFTER A COUPLE OF HOURS, PEOPLE WERE starting to leave, and I began to look around for Heather to make sure she didn't go back to her room yet. Troy was in on our surprise, and he was supposed to give us a fifteen minute head start so Brit, Julia, Alison, and I could get the suite ready before Heather got back.

Almost as if he sensed I was thinking about Heather's surprise party, Troy walked up to Jacob and me. We were seated in a quiet corner, talking and eating nongross food like brie and crackers.

"Heather's ready to go soon," he said. "I'll keep her here long enough for you guys to decorate."

"Thanks," I said, smiling at him.

Troy went back to Heather, and I turned to Jacob.

"I'm sorry," I said. "I have to go. If I don't get the decorations up in the Trio's suite, the surprise will be ruined."

Jacob rubbed his thumb over the top of my hand. "That's why you're my girlfriend. You're doing something nice for someone else." He helped me stand, and I wrapped my arms around his shoulders.

"I had a *wonderful* time," I said. "I'm so glad you came."

"Me too," Jacob said. He brushed his hand over my cheek. "I'm a lucky guy."

I smiled. "Yeah, you definitely are," I teased.

We kissed, longer this time, and I wished I could freeze this moment and stay here forever.

"Have fun with Heather's real party," he said. "I know you're going to make it a great night for her."

"Hope so." I smiled at him again, then let go of his hand as I walked away. I rounded up Brit and Alison, who were waiting near the door already alerted by Troy.

"Did you guys find Julia?" I asked.

Alison shook her head, her gold chandelier earrings bouncing off her neck. "Troy said he saw her with Ben, but we haven't seen her. I hope she didn't get sick or something or—"

"You guys ready?"

Julia, in a beautiful blue bandage dress, appeared in front of us, her arms folded across her chest.

"Ready, but where were you?" Alison asked. "I haven't seen you at all."

Julia glared at her. "I was with Ben. *Alone*, so we could talk. Okay? Geez. Any more questions?"

Alison looked as if she wanted to fire off another question, but she kept her mouth shut. "No. Let's go. Troy can only keep Heather busy for so long."

We sneaked out of the ballroom, hoping we wouldn't hear our phones start to go off if Heather realized we were all missing.

Racing across campus—well, as fast as we could in heels—we went back to Orchard. I went to my room to get the decorations and the present Brit and I had gone in on together for Heather. Once I got to the suite, Julia, Alison, Brit, and I raced to get everything the way we wanted it.

Brit put up streamers and the sign, I arranged the DVDs and snacks on the table, Alison poured giant cups of Coke, and Julia put the movie candy in bowls before sitting on the chair. Guess she was done.

"How's this look?" Brit asked.

"Perfect," I said. "I love how you spaced all the spirals—they look perfect."

Brit had grabbed a step ladder and taped the fun swirls to the living room ceiling. She'd also put the pink HAPPY BIRTHDAY!! sign across Heather's bedroom door.

"Presents!" Alison said. "Julia, grab yours and we'll put them on the table."

The girls went to their room and brought back two wrapped boxes. "I guess we got lucky that Heather's mom invited so many people," I said. "Heather had so many presents that she didn't even get to open—she didn't notice ours were missing."

My phone vibrated on the table. I opened a text from Troy.

H is on the way!

I wrote back.

We r ready. Thanks!

"She'll be here any second," I said. "Everyone ready?"

The other girls nodded. We got together around the couch, watching the door and waiting for Heather. She was probably furious—thinking we'd left her party without her.

Alison's phone buzzed. She looked at it, then back at us. "Heather's maaad," she said. "She thinks we all left her there and she wants to know where we are."

"Write her back that there was boy drama and we

didn't have time to explain, especially in front of Troy," Julia said. "So we came back to the suite."

"Good idea," Alison said. She typed and the phone buzzed seconds later. "She's on her way."

We stood, shifting from nervous excitement, as we waited for Heather. Keys turned in the lock and she walked in, fumbling with her purse.

"Whatever happened, there was no excuse for you guys to ditch me and—" Heather stopped midrant as she realized what was around her.

"Surprise!" we all yelled.

And, for the first time, Heather Fox was speechless.

"You—you guys," she finally said. "What is this?"

I reached behind the couch and handed her the admission ticket. "It's your birthday party. Your *real* party. The one you wanted."

Heather's cheeks flushed and she blinked, unsuccessfully trying to hold back a few tears.

"I can't believe you did this for me," Heather said. She looked around at the snacks, drinks, and decorations. "I had fun with Troy, I really did, but *this* is exactly what I wanted."

"Yay!" Alison said, hurrying over to hug her best friend. "We've got a ton of DVDs *and* Stephanie gave

Sasha and Brit permission to sleep over tonight, and we're allowed to stay up late."

"That's awesome," Heather said. "Really, really awesome. You guys have no idea how much this means to me. We're going to have the best night."

"We so are," I said. "The only thing that isn't here yet is the cake, but Stephanie's bringing that in a little while."

Brit handed Heather a stack of DVDs. "Are you ready for your thirteenth birthday party?"

Heather grinned. "So ready."

"Let's get into PJs, make some popcorn, and party," Julia said. She smiled at her friend and, for the first time in a while, her happiness looked genuine.

"Let's party!" Heather cheered.

I smiled as Heather took her movie ticket into her bedroom with her.

When Heather's door closed, Alison, Brit, Julia, and I high-fived. It looked like our party was going to trump Mrs. Fox's fancy, Manhattan-inspired soirée.

14

BLAST FROM
THE PAST

THE NEXT MORNING, I WOKE UP TO ALISON'S alarm clock. I'd slept in her room and Brit had stayed with Heather. I sat up, smiling as I thought about last night. Heather's party had been exactly what she'd wanted from the first DVD to the last. We'd stuffed ourselves with Junior Mints, Skittles, Dots, and soda. Stephanie had brought us a pizza and a lilac-colored cake fit for five, that had HAPPY BIRTHDAY, HEATHER! written in a beautiful font.

"Morning," Alison said, getting up and reaching for riding clothes in her closet. We had an early morning lesson to get to and, if she was anything like me, she was definitely still a little groggy from staying up late.

"Hey," I said. "I'm going to run back to my room in

my PJs, get dressed, and meet you, Julia, and Heather at the stable. Cool?"

"Definitely. I'll see you there."

I headed for the door.

"Sasha?"

I turned and Alison walked over and hugged me. "Thanks for helping give Heather such an awesome birthday."

"Of course," I said, hugging her back. "She's my friend—plus thirteen is a major deal. I think she got what she wanted."

Smiling, I left Alison's room. At the same time, Brit came out of the bathroom.

"You ready?" I asked. "We better go back to our room, get dressed, and go to the stable."

"Def."

We slipped on our flip-flops, and Heather emerged from her room in pink shorts and a white v-neck T-shirt. She walked up to us and got so close to me that I was afraid she was going to do something to me! And she did.

Heather reached out her arms and gave me a hug. It was the quickest hug in the history of hugs, but it was still bodily contact that wasn't, well, violent. She hugged

Brit, too, and smiled at both of us. She looked sleepy, with her normally straight hair a little tangled.

"Thank you both," she said. "I got exactly the birthday I wanted, thanks to you guys. I had the best birthday ever."

"You're welcome," Brit said.

"I'm glad you had a good birthday," I said. "Don't expect this kind of treatment every year." I stuck out my tongue at her, teasing.

Heather rolled her eyes with a hint of a smile and opened the door. "See you at the stable."

Brit and I left the suite and hurried to our room to get dressed and bundled up to go out in the cold morning air. That was my least favorite part of fall riding lessons—it took forever to throw on all the layers of clothes.

We walked down the sidewalk to the stables, and I noticed a silver horse trailer in the parking lot.

"They're not bringing trailers on campus yet for Huntington, are they?" I asked Brit.

She looked at the trailer, frowning. "I don't think so. It's kind of early."

A man got out of the truck cab and walked around to

the back of the trailer. Brit and I slowed, watching. He unlatched the door and stepped into the trailer. After a few seconds, a horse started to back out of the trailer. A gray mare stepped calmly out of the trailer, backing down the ramp and stepping onto the driveway. She was covered in a dark pink blanket with a matching halter and leg wraps.

"She's *gorgeous*," Brit said. "Wow. Almost perfect conformation."

"Yeah," I said slowly. "She's beautiful."

She looked familiar. But why? I had no idea where I'd seen her. Maybe a video or at another show.

"I bet she's a horse that Mr. Conner's going to work with once his leg is healed," I said.

"Ahhh," Brit said, nodding. "You're probably right."

The truck door with its tinted window opened and two black boots dangled above the pavement for a second before stepping onto the pavement. A willowy girl with long, wavy brown hair stepped around the truck door, closing it behind her and heading to the back of the trailer. She wore a hound's-tooth blazer, white breeches, and leather gloves. I squinted. She looked *so* familiar. But *no*, there was no way . . .

She took the lead line from the man and turned the

horse in the direction of the stable. I saw her face and I felt as if my heart fell to my boots.

"Sasha, c'mon," Brit said.

But I stood there. Watching.

The girl?

Lauren Towers.

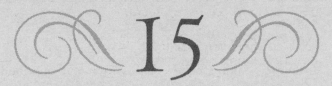

15

THE ONLY ONE WHO UNDERSTANDS

I TORE OFF TOWARD THE STABLE, FORCING Brit to run after me.

"Sasha," Brit called. "What's wrong? What happened?"

I grabbed her arm, pulling her into Charm's stall and locking us inside. I crouched down by his hay net so no one would see us, and Brit mimicked me.

Charm, obviously trying to give us away, ambled over, and started nuzzling us.

I put my head in my hands, feeling like I couldn't even comprehend what I was seeing.

"Talk to me," Brit said. "You've got some sort of history with that girl. Is she someone you met a show or something? Is she like Jasmine?"

I lifted my head slowly. "I have no idea if she's like

Jasmine and we've never officially met, but I saw her ride once."

"Who is she?" Brit asked.

I almost couldn't believe I was saying it out loud. "Her name is Lauren Towers. She's from Briar Creek."

"What?"

I nodded. "She's a year younger than us. I saw her ride when I went to visit Kim at my old stable—Briar Creek. She's a nationally ranked dressage star who started there after I left. Back then, it felt like she'd replaced me there." I paused, still trying to process. "And now, she's here."

"Try not to let her rattle you," Brit said. "She might become a great friend. You both have a history with Kim and Briar Creek. You could be the one to welcome her and really help her feel like she fits in."

"*I* just started to fit in," I said. "There's no way she'll want my help. Plus, it's just too weird. I'm not going to be mean or anything to her, I'm just going to stay out of her way."

Brit looked at me for a second, then stood. "Your call, obviously. I'm going to tack up Apollo, and I'll meet you in the arena."

"Okay, see you there."

I took out my phone and instinct took over. I typed a BBM.

Sasha Silver:

I had to talk to someone who would understand. Hope that's ok. Do u have a sec?

It only took her half a minute to respond.

Paige Parker:

Of course it's ok! What's going on?

Sasha Silver:

I was on the way to my riding lesson and I saw this horse and girl get out of a trailer and truck.

Paige Parker:

OMG. Pls, PLS don't tell me it was Jasmine.

Sasha Silver:

*Def not Jasmine. P, *Lauren Towers* is here.*

This time, it took Paige a minute to respond.

Paige Parker:

Lauren Towers. As in the younger rider from Briar Creek?

Sasha Silver:

Exactly.

Paige Parker:

Oh, Sasha. Whoa. What r u going 2 do?

Sasha Silver:

Stay away from her for now. I'm not in a place to be the

welcoming committee. And IDK, it kind of feels like she was my replacement at Briar Creek, even though I wanted to come here.

Paige Parker:

Def do whatever makes you comfortable. You don't know her though—she might turn out to be nice.

Sasha Silver:

We'll see. I'll keep you posted. C u in English.

Paige Parker:

Try 2 have a good lesson. And we'll talk more in class if u want.

I put my phone back in my pocket.

I looked both ways before I left Charm's stall, then hurried to gather his tack. I rushed through grooming and tacking him up, desperate to get to our lesson without running into Lauren.

I felt like I didn't breathe until I got into to the indoor arena and Mr. Conner hobbled inside, closing the door behind him and shutting Callie, Brit, Heather, and me inside.

He started to explain to us what we were going to do this morning, but I didn't hear his voice. Instantly, on repeat, I heard five words: *Lauren Towers is at Canterwood.*

16

HISTORY LESSON

"SILVER, YOU WERE A DISASTER," HEATHER said, shaking her head at me. We were cooling the horses in the arena after our lesson. Brit and Callie, who'd just finished, walked Apollo and Black Jack out of the arena.

"I think I'm allowed to be unfocused for one practice," I said. "Someone from *my* old stable, my old life is here. I left all of that behind to come to Canterwood, and now some younger, better dressage star decided to enroll."

"You're being a *little* dramatic," Heather said. "She's a *seventh* grader. Who. Cares. We're on the YENT. Who cares what Laura—"

"Lauren," I corrected her.

Heather glared at me. "As I was saying, who cares

what *Lauren* does when she's here. Nothing's changing for us, and no one's forcing you to start inviting her to sleepovers just because she's from Briar Creek."

I led Charm in another cooling circle. "You're right," I said, taking a deep breath. "I don't have to do anything. So what if she's here? I don't care."

With that, I led Charm out of the arena with Heather and Aristocrat close behind us.

An hour later, I'd made it to English class. But despite what I'd said earlier, I was still on constant lookout for Lauren—watching for her as I moved from class to class throughout the day. But I never saw her.

Brit and I headed back to our room after our last class of the day. Mr. Conner had canceled the afternoon lesson for a doctor appointment, and I'd decided not to practice again today—Charm deserved a break.

Brit and I got to our room and opened our backpacks, pulling out our homework.

"I think we're long overdue for a TV marathon, the second homework is done," Brit said.

"Could not agree more," I said.

We were twenty minutes into working when my phone rang. Heather's FaceSpace photo appeared on my phone.

"Hey," I said. "Don't tell me. Did Lauren move into the room next to you?"

"Sasha, drop the Lauren thing for five seconds," Heather snapped. Her voice was sharp and shaky at the same time.

"Are you okay?" I asked. "What's wrong?"

"You and Brit need to get over here. Right now."

"Okay, but why? What's going on?"

Heather didn't even answer my questions. The phone line went dead.

I shut my history book and got up.

"We've got to go to the Trio's suite right now," I said. "Something happened. I don't know what it is, but it's bad."

Brit was off her bed in a second. She and I put on flip-flops and hurried to the Trio's suite. I'd only knocked once when Heather yanked open the door. She locked it behind us and, without saying a word, motioned for us to follow her into Julia's bedroom.

Sitting on Julia's bed was a teary-eyed Alison.

"What *happened*?" I asked. "Where's Julia?

Heather stared out the window, then looked back at me. "She's at her book club. She won't be back for a while."

I was so confused. "Why are we in her room? And Alison, what's wrong?"

I sat beside her, putting a hand on her back.

Heather walked over to Julia's desk and picked up her laptop. She put it on the bed, motioning for Brit to sit by us.

Heather opened the laptop lid and woke it up out of sleep mode. The Canterwood gossip blog was pulled up.

I stared at it, frowning. "This is an old entry. I've already read it. I thought you guys had too."

Heather shook her head. "That's not why I pulled up this page." She clicked on Julia's Internet browser history and went to the last date a post had gone live. I didn't want to see what I was reading.

There were visits to Google, TMZ, a few gossip magazines and then, below those, were links to the Canterwood gossip blog.

Not the main page.

The *administration* page. Log in. Log out.

"No," the word came out like a moan from my throat. "There's no way that Julia did that. This has to be a mistake. Someone else used her computer. Something. This can't be true."

Brit's hand was on her forehead. "I can't believe this," she whispered.

"What can't you believe?"

Heather, Brit, Alison, and I jumped as Julia appeared in the doorway. We hadn't even heard her come in.

"What can't you believe?" Julia repeated, looking at us with an amused smile. Her eyes landed on the laptop. "Did you read something awesome online?"

Heather stood, walked over to Julia and stopped when the two were almost nose to nose.

"I did read something online," Heather said.

I'd never heard her voice like this. It sounded like she was choking back tears of sadness, disbelief, and a dozen other emotions. Julia looked at her, still not seeming to realize what had happened minutes before she'd arrived.

"I read," Heather continued, "your Internet history. I wish I'd known that the infamous Canterwood blogger was living in my suite."

Julia's face turned white. For a second, I thought she was going to crumble to the ground.

"Heather, listen, I was angry about the YENT. I started the blog and—" Julia started, but Heather cut her off with a wave of her hand.

"I don't care why you started it. What you did, what

you wrote—especially about your 'friends' was disgusting. Get out."

Julia shook her head. "What?"

Heather stared her down. "I said get out. Go straight to the headmistress's office and tell her everything."

Julia's eyes locked with Heather's. "No way. I'll be expelled for a stupid blog. I'll stop. I'll never write another word—I promise. Please just—"

This time, Julia stopped herself at the look on Heather's face.

"You go tell her now, or I'm giving her your laptop," Heather said. Her tone was deadly calm. "I will never be your friend again, and I don't want you living in this suite. You *will* get expelled. And you deserve it."

Heather stepped away from Julia, sitting in her desk chair. "I'm done talking. Go."

Julia's face turned a deep purple. Without a word, she turned walked out of the bedroom and slammed the door shut on her way out.

The four of us sat in silence.

For a long time.

That night, Brit and I were in our beds, reading. Kind of. It had been hours since the Julia incident, and we hadn't heard anything. We'd done our homework, but I hadn't been able to concentrate. I couldn't believe Julia had done this. Julia, part of the most powerful clique on campus, had lowered herself to a level I hadn't even known she was capable of. It felt as though I'd never known her at all.

My phone buzzed on my bedside table. I opened BBM and there was a single message.

Heather Fox:

Julia got expelled. She's already gone.

"Omigod," I said.

Brit sat up in bed. "Julia?"

I nodded as I typed back.

Sasha Silver:

Are you and Alison okay?

I waited for the message to deliver, but a red X appeared over the Heather's smiley face symbol. She'd turned off her phone.

I put mine down and turned to Brit, who was waiting.

I struggled to form the sentence. The words sounded weird in my head.

"Julia's gone."

17
REALLY GONE

FRIDAY FLEW BY IN A FLURRY. NEWS ABOUT Julia's abrupt departure spread all over campus. No one would stop talking about it. The only people who weren't, were Heather, Alison, Brit, and me. It was too soon—too raw. We'd all been betrayed by someone we'd considered a friend. I wasn't in a place to deal with it yet.

During the morning's riding lesson, Mr. Conner brought up Julia's absence. He talked about how he regretted that she felt it necessary to create the blog and do such harm to other people. He said that he hoped she sought help, so she could return to the student she had been and would one day fulfill her potential as an excellent rider. All of us had been quiet through Mr. Conner's speech and the lesson that followed.

I used it to distract myself from thinking about Julia. More than anything, I needed to focus on Huntington.

I moved through my classes in a daze, not hearing half of what the teachers said. None of them talked about Julia, but her absence felt ever present. I kept expecting to see her in the hallway or in one of the classrooms.

But she was really gone.

I walked across campus, back toward my dorm after my final lesson before Huntington. I'd managed to stay focused, and Charm and I had worked hard—with barely a misstep.

Jacob had BBMed me just as I'd finished grooming Charm.

Jacob Schwartz:

Are you hanging in there with the Julia situation? I'm so sorry, Sasha.

Sasha Silver:

I'm not great, but I'm trying 2 stay focused on 2mrw. I just don't understand how she could do this 2 us tho. Maybe 2 me since we were never superclose, but what abt Heather and Alison?

Jacob Schwartz:

People just snap sometimes. They lose perspective and do things you'd never think they're capable of. I think she needs some srs counseling, but I'm also not sorry she got expelled after what she did.

Sasha Silver:

U know what's sad? I'm not sorry abt that either—just that ppl got hurt.

Jacob Schwartz:

I know ur at the stable, but call me or BBM if u need 2 talk. I'm here.

Sasha Silver:

I know u r. Thank u.

I put away my phone and let Charm loose in his stall.

"Get some sleep, boy," I said. "I'll be here early tomorrow to get you ready to leave for Huntington."

I took my time walking back, almost unable to believe that the show was tomorrow. So many things had happened between when I'd started prepping for the show and now. Paige and I were on our way to being friends again, Callie and I were talking, Julia was gone, and Lauren was a new student.

Taking the long route, I passed through the courtyard and saw a girl with her back to me, sitting on a stone bench. It only took another step for me to realize who she was and what I had to do.

My boot heels clicked on the cobblestones, and I walked up to Lauren, careful not to startle her.

I stopped in front of the bench, staring down and then looking at her.

"Hi," I said.

Lauren looked back at me with big blue eyes. She'd pulled her long hair into a side ponytail, and she was dressed in a pea coat, lilac sweater, and boots with jeans tucked into them.

"I'm Sasha Silver," I continued.

"I know," Lauren's voice was soft. "You're *the* Sasha Silver from Union. From Briar Creek. It's so nice to meet you."

Lauren stood, stretching out her hand.

Formal, but with a smile.

I shook her hand and sat at the end of the bench. "And I know you too. I came to visit Briar Creek a long time ago, and I saw you jumping in a field. Kim told me about you and how great you were."

Lauren's fair skin blushed. "Not even close to you. Kim never stops talking about you. She uses your story as a way to encourage all of the riders at Briar Creek to look ahead and go for what we want."

"And you wanted to come to Canterwood?"

Lauren nodded, playing with her phone. "More than anything." She gave me a shy smile. "It's terrifying, but I have to try."

As she spoke, all of the jealousy of feeling as if she'd replaced me at Briar Creek and the anger I'd felt that she was here melted. Canterwood wasn't my territory. If I bullied Lauren or ignored her, I'd be no better than the Heather who'd tortured me for a long time when *I* first got here. I wouldn't trade even one experience away for another, and everything I'd gone through at Canterwood had made me the person I was today. A person I was proud to be. But that didn't mean that Lauren deserved to be threatened the way I'd been when I first got to Canterwood. And I wasn't going to be that person.

"Here," I said. "Put your number in my phone. Text me if you need anything, get lost, overwhelmed—whatever. You can talk to me anytime."

Lauren's entire face broke into a smile. "Really? That's so nice of you. You have no idea how much less nervous that makes me feel."

I got up. "Good. And seriously. Anytime."

I smiled at her and walked back to Orchard, ready to get a good night's sleep and prepare for tomorrow—Huntington.

18

IT'S SHOWTIME!

NO MATTER HOW MANY SHOWS I'D ATTENDED, they were all the same level of panicked frenzy. Brit and I had woken at four, dressed in sweats and made our way to the stable to groom our horses and prep them for the two-hour trailer ride.

At the stable, I followed my usual strategy of keeping Charm away from the craziness and in his stall until it was time to load.

I checked his leg wraps a final time, then let Mike lead him into the trailer next to Apollo.

"Everyone ready?" Mr. Conner asked. He was getting around faster every day on crutches, and I almost didn't even notice them anymore.

Callie, Brit, Heather, and I stood in front of him,

nodding. We'd already stored our show clothes in the truck's cab, and all of our tack was cleaned and loaded.

"Then let's go!" Mr. Conner smiled, and we followed him into the truck. He sat up front with Mike, who was driving. I sat next to Brit in the back row, and Heather and Callie sat together in the row in front of us.

We weren't even down the driveway before my head was resting on Brit's shoulder. In what felt like seconds later, Mr. Conner was calling back to us.

"Girls, we're here," he said.

Blinking, I lifted my head and looked out the window. The grounds were huge. We drove under a large sign above the driveway that said HUNTINGTON CLASSIC.

Dozens of horse and riders roamed the campus and there were giant horse trailers parked everywhere. For a second, I wondered if we'd even find a spot. But Mike, calm as ever, drove down until he found a wide spot for us unload our horses, tack them up, and not be sandwiched between trailers.

My phone buzzed, and I opened a text from Mom.

Hey hon!

Hope you all had a safe drive. Dad and I will be there soon. We don't want to distract you before your first class, but we'll be in the stands cheering you on. Love you! Mom & Dad

I was glad they were coming. Mr. and Mrs. Fox weren't, and Brit had said her parents were upset that they were both out of town on business trips that they couldn't cancel. But Callie's parents would both be here.

We unloaded the horses, who'd all been perfect passengers, and I tied Charm to the trailer.

Mr. Conner gathered us together once we'd secured our horses.

"Today, you're not getting the normal pep talk that you've heard a zillion times and probably makes you zone out the second I started talking," Mr. Conner said. "I want this to be brief so you can get in the warm-up ring and do what you do best—ride. I do want to remind you of one thing: you got to Huntington because of the quality of your riding, your dedication to the sport, and the level of commitment you've each displayed. You're all on the YENT because Mr. Nicholson and the other scouts saw potential in you just as I do. Think of today as a warm-up—a way to kick off the show season. Ride here the way you would at your home arena." Mr. Conner smiled at us. "And remember, that I'm here for you and am proud to have you representing Canterwood."

We smiled back, and I blinked, screaming to myself not to cry.

"Now, go get tacked up and warm up," Mr. Conner said. "Pick up your schedules from Mike and count on me to be there when your class begins. Good luck."

Mr. Conner walked away toward the sign-up tent, and Callie, Heather, Brit, and I stayed in line. Without a word or hesitation from anyone, we took the hand of the person next to us. We were a team.

Simultaneously, all of our phones buzzed, and we let go of each other and pulled them out of our pockets.

I opened a text.

So, I lied. Did you really think I was coming to some laaame schooling show? Puh-lease. You'll see enough of me @ shows that actually count. Be ready. ☺ *xoxo ~Jas*

"We all got the same message, right?" Heather asked.

Everyone nodded. We deleted the message, then started laughing. Even if Jasmine had showed, she couldn't have touched us. We'd become more than a team and *that* was something she didn't have.

An hour later, it was time for my first class—show jumping. I had an intermediate jumping class, basic dressage, lunch break, and finally, intermediate cross-country. We were all taking three classes, racking up points as individuals and for our school, but Mr. Conner had made us stick to beginner or intermediate level. He didn't want any of us to be overwhelmed at our first show of the season. Heather had a dressage class at the same time as me, and Mr. Conner was with her. I had no doubt that she would do well. Mike would be watching me, then Brit's show jumping round was next, while Mr. Conner stayed with me for dressage. But one thing at a time—I had to focus on my first class.

I'd taken Charm over several practice rails in the warm-up ring and he was *on*. He hadn't missed a step. We waited for the starting bell, and I kept my gaze in front of me and not on the people in the stands. I knew Mom and Dad were up there—I could feel them.

I settled myself into the saddle, ready to go the second the bell rang. *Diiing!* The bell chimed and I let Charm into the arena at a trot, then a steady canter. I'd been memorizing the jumping order since I'd gotten it, and I knew every jump we had to cover.

Charm's ears flicked back and forth as we approached the first of three verticals of increasing height. I wanted a clean ride, but I also wanted to watch our time. If we rode clean, I wanted to prevent a jump off.

Charm soared over the first red and white vertical.

And the second.

And the third.

We approached a faux stone wall, and I let him speed up to get enough momentum to clear it. He didn't hesitate for a second. He snapped his legs under him, clearing the stone with ease. Every bit of practice, the hours we'd spent in the arena, was paying off. We made a long curve around the arena, leaped a tall double oxer that Charm came *thisclose* to nicking. But he made it over. I let him speed up a hair more, and I stayed as still as possible in the saddle, letting him do his job.

Once afraid of creeks, Charm didn't slow over the liverpool. We made it over another vertical with vibrant tulips on both sides. I didn't let myself think about the fact that we were almost done. I had to stay focused.

We made another turn, and I checked the clock. Charm wasn't rushing, so I felt safe letting him speed up a tiny bit more. He didn't get greedy with the extra rein and kept his canter at a steady pace.

He wasn't sweating at all as we moved toward the final jumps. I rose out of the saddle before a blue-railed vertical, and Charm landed easily on the other side.

Two jumps left.

Charm was ready. I could feel it in his body. He jumped an oxer, meant to look like aged wood, without pause. We approached the final and tallest jump, a triple combination.

Charm cleared the first jump, took two strides, launched over the second, and I held my breath as we soared into the air over the third. It all happened so fast.

Cheers erupted from the crowd, and I patted his neck so hard, my hand stung.

"You were *amazing!*" I said. "I love you so much, boy."

Charm knew he'd done well. His trot had spring to it, and he moved toward the exit with his tail swishing with pride. There were fourteen riders after us, but I didn't care. Charm and I couldn't have done a better job.

We headed for the sidelines to wait for results.

"Beautiful, Sasha," Mike said, coming up to us. He helped me loosen Charm's girth and patted his shoulder. "That was one of your best, if not the best, ride you've ever given."

"Thank you," I said.

I decided not to watch the other riders, it would only make me more nervous.

"I'm going to take Charm for a walk," I told Mike. "But we'll be back before the results."

"Enjoy," he said. "You both deserve it."

I led Charm out of the arena and back to a quiet

pasture. The rest of the riders were in class or warming up. It felt good to have time to ourselves. We stayed outside for what felt like half an hour before I decided it was time to go back so we didn't chance missing the ribbon ceremony.

I led Charm back inside and spotted Mike in the same spot by the rail. Almost afraid to look, I glanced up at the scoreboard.

"What?" I asked Mike.

"You have the best time and *every* rider has made a mistake," Mike said. "The last rider is in the arena now. Sasha, you'll either be first or second."

I watched a guy take his gray mare over the final jumps and, almost as if he was showing off, he forced her into a near gallop for the last jump. The mare was too rushed and her knees knocked the rail.

Oh.

My.

God.

"Congratulations!" Mike said, patting my shoulder. "You and Charm won."

"No. Way," I said. "No way!"

I scanned the stands, looking for my parents. I finally spotted them, a pair of green and gold human pom-poms.

They were standing and screaming for me. I waved at them and grabbed Charm in a hug.

After a few minutes, one of the judges called the top riders into the ring. I couldn't stop smiling when the judge reached Charm and me.

"Congratulations, Miss Silver," he said. He pinned a blue ribbon Charm's bridle and reached up to shake my hand.

"Thank you, sir," I said.

In that moment, my anxiety about my other classes disappeared. I would do my best in dressage, and Charm and I would attack cross-country. The pressure of I-have-to-win-because-I'm-on-the-YENT disappeared.

I'd finally learned what it meant to be a complete horse lover, not just a rider. I beamed from Charm's back, soaking in the moment not only of victory, but of being with my horse and friends, doing what I loved.

19

PASSING THE GLOSS

THE SUN STARTED TO SINK BEHIND THE rolling hills of the campus as I led Charm up a grassy lane. Before I went home for Thanksgiving break, I wanted to spend time with him. It was chilly in the November air, and I'd bundled him in a quilted green blanket. He walked in step with me, not bounding ahead as he usually did.

"You're still a little tired from the show yesterday, huh?" I asked him.

Our win in show jumping had been the most amazing feeling. We'd placed fourth in our dressage class, and instead of being disappointed, I'd been proud because I knew we'd tried our hardest.

The most exciting round for us had been cross-country. The course, simple compared to what Mr.

Conner put us through, had barely made Charm work up a sweat. We'd come in well under time and without a mistake. We'd even been faster than Heather and Aristocrat, who had been in our class. We'd secured first and second for Canterwood. Heather had won her show-jumping round, and Brit, as if it was ever a doubt, had stolen the blue ribbon for her dressage class.

At the end of the show day, all of our individual points had been tallied. We'd been three points behind Pershing Preparatory, and they'd taken the win. By one point, we'd secured second place. Heather, Callie, Brit, and I had waited until we'd gotten to the truck cab to scream and hug each other.

Competition would never get any easier. Soon, we'd be up against Wellington and Jasmine. Pershing Prep was a tough school to beat, and we knew where we needed to get better. But we had *all* season to work together as a team. Knowing that Callie and I were riding together and speaking again, that Heather and I could ride in the arena without killing each other, and that I had Brit there meant the most. I was *beyond* thrilled about this season.

Maybe even more exciting? I was meeting Paige at The Sweet Shoppe for dessert after my walk with Charm. I couldn't wait for our usual brownies and hot chocolate.

Charm and I walked up the path that led up a gentle hill. It felt like we were the only horse and rider on campus—a feeling that didn't happen too often since the school was always nonstop busy.

As we walked, I reveled in the cool air and being with Charm. I couldn't help but think back to when I'd first come to Canterwood. It made me smile. Then, my main goals had been to survive the Trio, make the advanced team, and not flunk out of any of my supertough classes. Things had changed a lot since I'd come here.

"I almost can't even believe where we are now, boy," I said to Charm. "We're on the YENT, I'm with Jacob, and maybe everything's going to start to calm down." I paused, laughing to myself. There was no way *that* part was true. Classes were always going to be grueling, Heather was still going to be my friend slash sometimes-frenemy, and Charm and I were going to have to work harder than ever to keep our place on the YENT. But the more I thought about it, the more I realized that I wouldn't have it any other way. The craziness of Canterwood kept things interesting.

"Oh!" I halted Charm, startled by the girl in front of me. Lauren Towers.

Her light brown hair was loose and wavy around her

shoulders, and she looked classic-chic in white breeches, a brown jacket, and a hunter green shirt. I loved the pale pink rose with gold edges that hung around her neck.

"Hey," I said.

"Hi," Lauren said, halting her horse. The gray mare stretched her muzzle toward Charm. The two of them seemed to sense a connection—maybe they knew that Lauren and I were both from Union and that Lauren had trained at Briar Creek, too.

"What's her name?" I asked, nodding at Lauren's horse.

"This is Whisper," she said. "And I already know the famous Mr. Charm." She reached out a hand to stroke his shoulder. He leaned into her touch—something he rarely did with strangers. He liked her.

"How's everything going so far?" I asked.

Lauren touched her necklace. "Really well, actually. I'm still getting used to classes, obviously, and Whisper's adjusting to being here."

"It seems like you're fitting right in. I'm glad you're here."

That made Lauren smile.

"That means a lot coming from you," she said.

I cocked my head, looking at her. "What are you talking about?"

Lauren looked at me as if I should have known.

"You're a celebrity in Union. Like an actress who left home and made it big in LA or something. Everyone at Briar Creek knows that you started there and ended up at Canterwood. You're kind of my—"

She blushed.

I waited, not pressing her.

"You're kind of my idol," Lauren said. "And I don't mean that in a fan-girly oh-my-God-it's-Sasha-Silver way. I just mean that I think it's pretty cool that you got from Briar Creek to here."

I shook my head. "No way am I anyone's idol. I've messed up *so* many times since I've been here. I should win some kind of award for that."

We both laughed.

"Want to walk the horses up to the top of the hill?" I asked Lauren.

She nodded. "If you don't mind."

She adjusted the strap on Whisper's pink blanket and we walked the short distance up the hill. The horses' breaths became visible in the ever cooling air.

Lauren, Whisper, Charm, and I reached the top of the hill and we stopped. I stared across the campus—taking in the gentle glow of the streetlamps that had flickered on and the lights that shone from windows of the dorm buildings.

In the big outdoor arena, Heather was taking Aristocrat over a round of jumps while Alison and Brit, also on horseback, looked as if they were coaching Heather.

Callie, at the opposite end, moved Black Jack through gorgeous serpentines. Relationships among all of us may have changed, but we were still teammates and that was *my* team practicing.

I looked at Orchard, my new home with Brit, and then stared at Winchester on the other side of campus. Both places felt like home and *that* was the biggest relief—to have my relationship back with Paige even if we weren't living together. But who knew about the future. Maybe we'd share a triple with Brit next semester.

The possibilities were endless.

I turned to Lauren. "So, you're the new girl from Union now. Not me."

Lauren's eyes flickered—she looked nervous. "I didn't come here to take anything away from you—I swear. I—"

I touched her shoulder. "I'm not talking about that at all. I'm trying to say that I'm glad to have someone else from my hometown here. We Union girls have to stick together."

I could see Lauren's smile even in the fading sunlight.

"I like that," she said. "Team Union all the way."

I reached into my pocket, pulling out something I'd been carrying for days.

"Here." I handed Lauren a brand new Watermelon Lip Smackers. "It's my fave flavor."

"Sasha!" Lauren took the gloss, grinning. "Thank you. I know how much you love your gloss."

"So my obsession has gotten around, huh?" I laughed. "It's kind of a welcome-to-Canterwood present, but more of a passing-the-torch sort of thing, I guess. You're the new girl now. I'll be in high school next year, and it'll be up to you to represent. I know you can do it."

Lauren locked eyes with me—hers wide. "Thank you." Her voice was quiet. "I'll do the best I can—I promise. Union girls *do* have to stick together."

We didn't say another word—nothing else needed to be said. Together, we watched the orange-red sun set over Canterwood Crest.

ABOUT THE AUTHOR

Twenty-three-year-old Jessica Burkhart is a writer from New York City. Like Sasha, she's crazy about horses, lip gloss, and all things pink and sparkly. Jess was an equestrian and had a horse like Charm before she started writing. To watch Jess's vlogs and read her blog, visit www.jessicaburkhart.com.

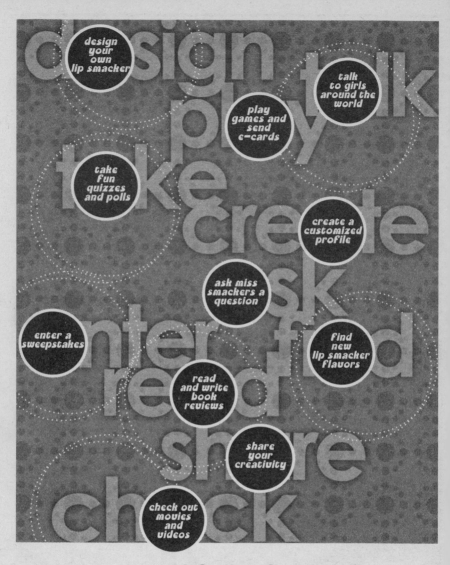

Jammed full of surprises!

LiP SMACKER®

LOUNGE

VISIT US AT WWW.LIPSMACKERLOUNGE.COM!

FIVE GIRLS. ONE ACADEMY. AND SOME SERIOUS ATTITUDE.

CANTERWOOD CREST

by Jessica Burkhart

TAKE THE REINS
BOOK 1

CHASING BLUE
BOOK 2

BEHIND THE BIT
BOOK 3

TRIPLE FAULT
BOOK 4

BEST ENEMIES
BOOK 5

LITTLE WHITE LIES
BOOK 6

RIVAL REVENGE
BOOK 7

HOME SWEET DRAMA
BOOK 8

CITY SECRETS
BOOK 9

Don't forget to check out the website for downloadables, quizzes, author vlogs, and more!

www.canterwoodcrest.com

FROM ALADDIN M!X   PUBLISHED BY SIMON & SCHUSTER